Belinda Blinked 2;

The continuing story of, dripping sex, passion and big business deals;

Keep following the sexiest sales girl in business as she continues to earn her huge bonus by being the best at removing her silk blouse.

Author; Rocky Flintstone;

Belinda Blinked 1; is also a published book. It's incorporated in the podcast version called My Dad Wrote a Porno now available in Europe on this link....

http://bit.ly/MDWAP

And in the USA on this link....

http://amzn.to/2zjVmmF

Contents;

Chapter 1

Ritz Spa Gossip;

Belinda's phone rang.

'Belinda here.' she answered.

'It's Tony, get your ass into my office pronto!'

'Yes sir, on the double!' replied Belinda feeling distinctly upset. After all she'd done for the company yesterday, she didn't need to be treated like the office cat. But it was Tony the MD, so she'd better get along quickish.

Two minutes later Belinda was standing outside Tony's door. She mentally steeled herself and knocked.

'Come in!' answered a gruff voice. 'Ahh Belinda, that was fast, sit down.'

Belinda did as she was told, still furious at his demeanor to her. He passed her a fax and said,

'What do you make of that?'

It was an official order from Peter Rouse's supermarket company for 5,000 units of utensils.

'Fantastic!' breathed Belinda.

'Belinda it's not fantastic, it's bloody unbelievable... what did you do with him yesterday afternoon in that bloody maze?'

'Ahh... that would be a professional secret Mr. MD sir!' replied Belinda.

'Well it's a sweet deal for the company, we've had some of these units in stock for at least 6 months, and this will clear our inventory very nicely!'

'But the quality is still good Tony?' said Belinda fearing they were going to sell Rouse's organisation a pup.

'The best of course, it's just our sales force can't get any outlets for them, but thinking on it, perhaps the continent is where we should have been selling them in the first place.'

'Great!' said Belinda, 'I'm in Amsterdam this Thursday and Friday to tie up the loose ends with Peter so I'll keep in touch on this one.'

'Meeting now officially over!' said Tony.

Belinda left the office feeling stunned; it wasn't every Monday morning a new major client came on board, whatever next?

Back in Belinda's office, Giselle popped her head round the door and said to Belinda, 'He's given us some free passes to the Ritz, so why not come with me today to the Spa!'

'Thanks Giselle... that's fantastic!' Belinda grinned, 'come on, let's get out of here... pronto!'

The Ritz Spa was in central London near Knightsbridge so the two girls took the tube. At the Spa entrance they passed over their admission cards and let everything just happen. The cards were of

VIP status and they were immediately led to a lounge serving champagne. They left their valuables in a small room where they also changed into white robes and collected three large towels each. A staff member then guided them to the mud room.

'Dear ladies, we are honoured to have you join us today, please feel free to ask for refills or anything else that you might desire. First you will experience the mud room, then the saunas, then the crystal pools and finally the beauty salons. The whole process takes around five hours, so lunch will be served when you want it. Afternoon tea and snacks are also available. At the end of your course we hope you will be relaxed and refreshed, ready to go back to the rigors of your daily life!'

Belinda and Giselle looked at each other.

'Plenty of time to chat then.' said Giselle.

'Lots to hear I think.' replied Belinda.

Giselle relaxed into her mud pack and sipped her champagne thoughtfully.

'Belinda, do you mind if I tell you everything, I mean even the stuff I kept from Tony.'

'Giselle, if it means that much to you, then I'd be honoured.' said Belinda. 'So spill the beans.'

'Well as you know, just after the BBQ, Tony placed you in the maze. He then took me to the building which houses Sir James' antique cars. It's quite large and in the centre there was a four poster bed.

Tony tethered me to the four poster with some ridiculously pink coloured plastic handcuffs.'

Belinda nodded, she knew only too well this scenario.

'He told me he would be back in two hours and to enjoy the bed. Nothing happened for the first hour and I thought, well, fun party that hasn't happened, at least I'm comfortable here on this posh bed. Then I heard the singing...'

'What do you mean singing?' asked Belinda now intensely interested.

'It was an old Irish song called, 'Will you go lassie go.'

'How very apt.' said Belinda.

'Yes, they sang it really well, all in harmony, they have great voices of course.'

'If I didn't know you better, I'd say you were suffering from a type of Stockholm syndrome.' mused Belinda. 'How many of them did you say there were?'

'Ahh my first confession Belinda, I told Tony there were six of them, but actually there were only three.'

Belinda let a slow whistle emit through her teeth and thought, six would have definitely been better than three.

'So they marched into the building between the cars and up to the bed where I was sitting naked, they reminded me a bit of the seven dwarfs, they always went everywhere in a line. All they were wearing was a black thong, so it didn't take long for them to get ready for action. Well then they started to kiss me all over and eventually one of them called Kevin started to lick my pussy. Another called Danny massaged my tits and a third called Sean kissed my ass.'

Belinda wondered what Giselle was missing out, it all sounded terribly civilized, and she reckoned she had had a harder time in the Maze. Belinda said nothing and just nodded.

'This all lasted for about ten minutes with a bit of rotation going on between the lads. Between you and me, Danny was the best at licking my clit, though I never said anything as I didn't want to upset any of them... I mean they were all good, but he was definitely the best.'

Belinda started to wonder what Giselle was trying to say, did she fancy Danny?

'In the meantime of course I started to pump their cocks with both hands, it was an easy decision to make who got what as the one kissing my ass was out of reach, so they missed out, I think that's why they started to rotate, if you get my meaning.'

Belinda nodded her head again and thought, 'yes, I'd get a bit upset if I only had the rump and no stimulation.'

'Besides, Danny's cock was really responding big time so I started to give him a blow job, and that sent the other two scrambling for my tits and clit. Danny got a hold of my hair and started to twist it whilst I continued working his cock down my throat, he really enjoyed that and came the next minute. I think that's when the scuffle broke out between the other two, you know, in their rush to get their cocks into my mouth. Anyway, they only landed a couple of punches on each other with Sean coming off the worst, he must have a beautiful black eye today thinking about it.'

Giselle laughed and Belinda grimaced slightly, she couldn't believe what she was hearing.

'Is that how you got your limp?' asked Belinda.

'No, but I'll come to that bit later. As I said, Kevin won the tussle for the next blow job and I duly obliged him, he wasn't as turned on as Danny, probably the punch to his lip from Sean didn't help, but you know me Belinda, I never admit defeat and I got him to respond after a few minutes of prick teasing with my tongue and lips. Once he was up, it was child's play to complete the job and he came quickly. That only left Sean who hadn't had an ejaculation at this point of the session, so in all fairness I had to concentrate on him.'

At that point the spa assistants came out of a side room and approached the two girls.

'Ladies, it's time to remove the mud packs please and then we'll get you to the sauna area.'

Giselle and Belinda fell silent and enjoyed the mud pack removal process which only took a few minutes and with their robes on they were led down a corridor to the sauna area. The assistant poured out some champagne into two fancy delicately cut flutes, put two small white towels on their chairs and disappeared into a side room.

'This is great,' said Belinda, 'I could certainly get used to this standard of gym very easily.'

'Cheers Belinda,' said Giselle as she knocked back her champagne in one go.

'And you too Giselle, here's to a happy ending to your story.' Belinda followed Giselle's lead and knocked back her drink. Giselle got up and took the bottle out of the cooler and poured another two drinks.

'Let's take these into the steam room and get started, these glasses are actually very posh plastic, so they won't break,' said Giselle, 'and bring that small towel so you can sit on it.'

Belinda followed Giselle, who was still limping, across the central area into the first cubicle.

Belinda opened the glass door and let Giselle limp into the steam. They put down their towels and glasses next to each other and waited for their eyes to accustom to the murky interior. Already inside were two well-tanned ladies with fantastic asses and good sized tits. They were around thirty five years old and obviously enjoying each other's company. Oblivious to the newcomers, they were kissing and fondling each other's breasts with some enthusiasm. Giselle looked at Belinda and Belinda looked at Giselle. If you can't beat 'em join 'em was the phrase which came to both their minds. Without further ado, Giselle kissed Belinda full in the mouth and Belinda responded by touching Giselle's nipples. Belinda softly moaned as Giselle's hand snaked down to her clitoris and she opened her legs just a touch to allow Giselle further access. In return Belinda took one hand away from Giselle's breast and traced a line down her body to her vagina. With a deft movement, she pulled her lips apart and found her hot spot. The small nub of flesh became wet extremely quickly, no doubt helped by the invasive steam.

Giselle murmured softly in Belinda's ear after a few moments,

'This is not the place.'

Belinda nodded, sat back and sipped at her champagne. Giselle did the same and they watched the other two women for any sign of acknowledgement. None came, everyone's privacy was intact and after a few more minutes, Belinda and Giselle decided to have lunch.

Belinda directed the conversation over lunch back to a question she had been meaning to ask all morning.

'What was the name of the organization these Irishmen worked for Giselle?'

'Ahaa... Belinda the business woman appears.' laughed Giselle. 'What would you say if I didn't know... well don't answer that as I'm only teasing you!'

Belinda pulled a face and stuck her very sweet tongue out at Giselle.

'Okay, okay, McDonagh Brothers, from Dublin, they have six cash and carries throughout Ireland with another seven in Boston and Chicago. Very well established and definitely of interest to us. They already do some business with us but nowhere near their full potential.'

'That's the story of this company we work for.' replied Belinda.

Giselle nodded and poured another two flutes of champagne.

'Yes, and with my assistance, I reckon we can get them on board.'

'We… don't you mean Me, or are you taking over sales as well as Tony's job.' replied Belinda.

'Belinda, I mean we… you and me… the team!'

'Okay, I understand, and thanks, I've always found it hard to tie down the Irish, they tend to squirm so much!

'Just like a worm,' replied Giselle.

'And speaking of which,' interrupted Belinda, how did you lose your hair?'

'Well Belinda, I have to admit, I got fucked so hard some of my hair fell out…it's a genetial disease I've inherited from my mother. That was the only distressing part of the whole afternoon… I'd lost my beautiful blonde hair style; it'll take months to get those curves back.'

Giselle fell silent. Belinda, put a hand on hers and said,

'You know… it suits you this shorter hair,' ('well no hair,' thought Belinda rolling her eyes,) 'Okay, it could be more curvy, but it's really modern… a statement!

Giselle smiled and said, 'Thank you dear friend.'

'But what I don't understand is your limp.'

Giselle blushed, 'I slipped on a pool of semen and wrenched my ankle.'

Belinda said, 'How terrible Giselle, you could have broken your arm or worse still bruised your tits.'

Giselle nodded, shivered and said, 'You won't tell Tony all the truth, will you? I don't want him to think I'm clumsy or know I have a genetic defect.'

'Giselle, I'm your friend, we have each other's backs, besides, I smell another multi-million dollar deal in the pipeline.'

They both laughed and Belinda thought, I'm not going to ask you about Danny McDonagh, it could be too personal, and too early.

Chapter 2;

Amsterdammmm;

The tyres of the Cityjet, squealed only once as Belinda touched down at Schiphol airport, it was a text book landing and Belinda hoped it was a good omen for her short trip. After collecting her lone suitcase from the baggage hall (was everyone travelling light these days?) she made her way to the airport exit. A short fat man with a sign saying Blumenthal was leaning against one of the pillars, a wary Belinda approached him and asked the obvious question… 'Are you waiting for me?'

'If you're from Steele's Pots and Pans and you're called Blumenthal, then yeah!'

'Wow! That's great, yes I'm Belinda Blumenthal and I've got a 4.00pm appointment with your purchasing director Dr. Robbins.'

'Good, and yes you have, let me take your bags and follow me to the car. Might I say as a word of welcome to the company, what fantastic breasts and legs you have.'

Belinda smiled back at him wondering if she should show a bit of nipple as a sign of appreciation… were all Dutch men as forward as this?

Thirty minutes later they pulled into a reserved parking space outside a nondescript, but very old building in the canal district of Amsterdam. She adjusted her brassiere making sure she covered her wonderful nipples, which the chauffeur had been inspecting during the drive, and pulled her blouse back over her breasts. She didn't really want to create a bad first impression with all of Peter's staff. The high Dutch gables overlooked the very famous Herengracht (Gentlemen's) canal. In a past life it was obviously a merchant's warehouse, but today it had been converted to the exclusive head office of Peter Rouse's international company where only the executive directors were quartered.

The driver opened the car door and Belinda stepped out, making sure he saw a long length of thigh with just a peek of thong and thanked the driver once again. She strode boldly across the pavement and entered through the antique wooden double doors. The driver had been instructed to take her suitcase to the upmarket Ambassade Hotel just a few minutes walk away from the offices. Here Peter Rouse had reserved one of their exclusive Presidential rooms for her use during her short trip.

Belinda walked across to reception and passed her business card to the pretty blonde lady who was behind the desk. Belinda studied her as she operated the computer, she reckoned she was about 36 and a natural blonde, the outline of a tight ass peeked out from a knee length business skirt, and the legs looked half decent. Hmm Belinda thought 'nice body.'

'I have an appointment with Dr. Robbins at 4.00 pm.' Belinda informed the receptionist. She replied by confirming,

'Ms. Blumenthal of Steele's Pots and Pans?'

Belinda grimaced, she just couldn't get used to the corny name of her parent company.

'Yes, that's me.'

'Thank you, please follow me. We'll take the elevator to the first floor and I'll sign you in at that floors reception. Sorry about all the security, but we do get the occasional terrorist threat from time to time as we're a pretty high profile company. Dr Robbins has been notified you are in the building.'

Belinda walked across to the lift glancing at the gently swinging rear end in front of her. Belinda felt a twang deep between her own long legs. She pursed her lips and blew a quick kiss which she knew the receptionist couldn't possibly see. However unluckily for Belinda she turned round at that precise moment. The blonde blushed, the lift chimed and the doors opened. The journey to the first floor was uneventful apart from the creaking and straining of the 1930's era lift. Then the lift suddenly shuddered to a halt and the lights dimmed to half power, Belinda thought it was possibly a power cut... surely not a terrorist attack?

The blonde looked at Belinda and said, 'Don't be worried, these old lifts do this all the time, the doors will open in a few minutes.' She then started to remove her jacket, 'It does get hot in here very quickly, you may want to do the same!' Belinda followed suit and unfastened her blouse casually.

'Let me help you with that.' the blonde receptionist said. She expertly undid the rest of Belinda's blouse and uncoupled her bra. Belinda's tits fell out, the blonde lady gasped.

'You have exceptional breasts Belinda, may I call you that?'

'Only if you tell me your name and let me see your naked ass.' replied Belinda smiling.

'I'm Cristina, and here's my ass!' Cristina quickly pulled down her skirt and knickers and bent over to allow Belinda to rub her tits over her ass cheeks. In doing so Belinda grasped Cristina's tits, Cristina stood up and pulled off her blouse and bra, she was now virtually naked. She was a magnificent well-tanned creature, perfectly honed in every way and obviously spent all her spare time in the gym. Cristina pulled Belinda's skirt down and relieved her of her thong. The two girls played with each other's naked bodies and started kissing. The lift jolted.

'Oh ho', Cristina said, 'we'd better get dressed, these lift doors will open up in about a minute. The two girls scrambled to put on their clothes, and had virtually finished just as the lift restarted and the doors opened. They both smoothed back their hair, composed themselves and walked out of the lift as if nothing had happened.

Now safely on the first floor, Cristina signed Belinda in and left her to wait for Dr. Robbins in the beautifully decorated visitor's area. Five minutes later a middle aged gent exited from one of the doorways fronting onto the canal. He walked quietly down the corridor towards Belinda. He was quite oddly dressed for a Dutchman as he was covered in Harris Tweed with brown brogues on his feet. He looked more like a Scottish MP than a very successful purchasing director. His face smiled when he saw Belinda and gestured her to follow him.

'Ms Blumenthal, I presume?'

'Yes sir,' Belinda replied, 'and I take it that you are Dr Robbins?'

'Indeed the very same.' he replied still smiling. 'Peter Rouse has told me a lot about you, but he did admit I would have to find out myself how you tick… if you see what I mean!'

Belinda smiled, 'Yes, Peter did send me a quick itinerary this morning of my time in Amsterdam and I know I have a full two hours discussing contracts with you.'

'And very boring it will be too, but we do have to do these things don't we Belinda, may I call you that?'

'Why yes of course, I wouldn't dream of you calling me anything else!'

Now here we are, please step into my world.' Robbins opened one of the few doors lining the corridor and ushered Belinda inside. Belinda gasped, the office was full of ancient furniture and wall hangings of erotic art but the centre piece was an extremely large wooden oak desk with a stunning red leather top. It must have been two hundred years old and looked well used with many contractual papers strewn across it. Behind it was one of the original warehouse windows facing the canal, through which streamed glorious sunshine from the strong afternoon sun. Robbins waved to a chair at the far side of the room and perched himself in front of Belinda on the edge of his desk.

'Now,' Robbins said, 'As you know, we have made our first order.' At that moment a previously hidden side door to the office opened and a bespectacled, frumpily dressed, middle aged, but still somewhat attractive secretary, entered the room with an armful of papers.

'Ahh, Helga, thank you, these are the contracts for this morning's meeting I take it?'

' Ja meneer, Dr. Robbins.' Helga put the papers down, nodded at Belinda and went back into what must have been her office area.

Robbins then purposely moved to the other side of the desk, as if he had decided on something and quickly tidied away the papers strewn across it, placing them beside the pile Helga had left for his attention.

He coughed, 'Belinda, this sunlight is unseasonably harsh, would you like to remove your jacket... you must be feeling hot?'

Belinda thought for a split second and answered, 'Yes, and would you mind if I loosened a few of my blouse buttons at the same time?'

'No, not at all, we're all adults here...' and he laughed in a high pitched effeminate way.

Belinda took off her jacket and unfastened two buttons at the top of her cream coloured blouse and two at the bottom. This left only one which was now being quite unfairly challenged by her ample breasts, even though they were being adequately contained by her brassiere.

Dr. Robbins sat back in his office chair and appraised the now slightly uncomfortable Belinda. He thought to himself, 'I very much like what I see and Peter did ask me to challenge her, I think I will put her to the complete test... one I reserve only for our biggest suppliers and see what happens.'

Robbins coughed again and this time he asked Belinda to move her chair directly into the strong sunlight. Belinda obliged immediately, she always enjoyed a bit of heat.

'Before we discuss the contracts I would like to offer you a glass of our traditional drink called, Jenever... it's basically our gin but with a very strong Juniper berry taste.' The Doctor got up and went to one of the many cabinets lining the walls. He handed Belinda a large glass of the pale white liquid and sat down with his in his chair.

'Proost!' he exclaimed and knocked it down in one. This was territory Belinda knew well from her university years and she followed suit. Robbins got up and refilled the glasses; once again the procedure was followed.

'Now...' he said, 'are you relaxing Belinda?'

Belinda Blinked;

She smiled, she knew exactly what was coming next, but she very much wanted to tie up the contracts, so she decided to make things easier for the very shy Doctor.

'Dr. Robbins, would you mind very much if I removed my high heels... they've been killing me all day...'

'Belinda, Belinda,' Robbins replied, 'you have no need to ask... why you can remove your stockings if you so desire!'

Belinda smiled and said, 'You are so, so understanding!'

Chapter 3;

The Dutchman's leather desk;

The sunlight was declining now and Belinda still couldn't work out how Robbins had managed to manipulate her onto his red leather desk where she now sat cross legged. She had to admit that she hadn't lost any more of her clothing, but then all she was wearing was her nearly fully open blouse, a bra, a thong and a skirt. She had willingly discarded the rest of her clothing in Robbins office even before they had discussed the contracts. Now the good Doctor was sitting opposite her with his head on one side appraising her body.

'Belinda, you look very hot, would you like to remove your blouse... I certainly don't mind in the least... you'll feel more relaxed I'm sure.'

Belinda smiled again and with the hint of a very small tease she undid the last button holding her cream blouse in place. She then slowly removed it from her arms and back and tossed it towards the small pile of clothing now accumulating with her high heels, behind her. Robbins let out a long sigh, Belinda's breasts, even though they were still modestly concealed by her brassiere, were to say the least, magnificent, indeed he had to admit to himself they were probably the best he had ever seen in real life. Of course he understood she couldn't compete with the many large busted girls on the web, but that was irrelevant in the here and now. How he envied his Managing Director Peter Rouse.

By this time the five o clock sun and the two very strong Jenevers were getting to Belinda. She was starting to sweat out the gin, albeit gently. She decided to up the pace and asked Dr Robbins, 'Would you really mind if I removed my skirt... it's rather tight in this cross legged position and I would like to stretch my legs and feel the smooth leather of your desk on my skin.

'Yes, do what you need to Belinda... your comfort in this office is my ultimate concern.' Robbins high pitched laugh once again escaped from his effeminate mouth. Belinda got onto her knees, wriggled her ass and removed the garment in one smooth motion.

'My, that was graceful!' exclaimed the Doctor as Belinda calmly tossed the skirt over her back. Dressed only in her, perhaps, real working clothes, as she would sometimes unfairly put it to Giselle back in London, Belinda re-crossed her legs and waited for Robbins to make the next move. It didn't take long, and it wasn't what Belinda had ever experienced before in any of her sexual adventures.

Belinda shut her eyes and relaxed in the sunshine, she felt strangely uplifted, she had a feeling things were at last going her way. Robbins was obviously strange, but so far he had been utterly harmless, if not charming and it certainly wasn't his fault he was odd. Indeed most of her best friends in London were unusual people and it didn't really matter as they were all good fun and would help you out if you ever had a problem. Besides, Belinda didn't do boring in any part of her life.

It came as a bit of a shock when Belinda reopened her eyes to see Dr. Robbins with a pair of long handled surgical scissors in his hands. She stifled her gasp, but couldn't control her breasts from heaving up and down as she breathed more rapidly.

'Don't worry my dear, this will not hurt you one little bit.' as he pointed them towards her breasts, still hidden beneath her brassiere. With one swift movement the Doctor cut through the loop of fabric attaching the two cups of her cream lace bra together. Released from the confining effects of her bra, Belinda's tits fell forwards. Her nipples immediately started to harden as they felt the warmth of the sunlight. The Doctor then turned his attention to her black lace thong, again with two precise cuts, one on either side of her long thigh's and the thong fell uselessly onto the red leather desk revealing her flushed vagina for Robbins to see.

But Robbins had no time to view his work as he quickly put the scissors away in his desk drawer and immediately took out a similar styled pair of surgical tweezers. Belinda was in shock, she'd quickly gotten over the scissors, but tweezers? Again she needed not have worried as the good Doctor pinched her flapping lace bra and roughly pulled it off her back. He threw it to the floor and concentrated on Belinda's now quite useless thong. With the same sure actions it was soon disposed of, albeit with a bit of consensual movement from Belinda's now quite naked ass.

The setting sun continued to beat down on a reddening Belinda as she sat cross legged on the antique leather desk. Completely naked, Belinda wondered how this scenario would end. At no point during her time with the Purchasing Director had he touched her physically, except for a token handshake when they had first met. Time would tell, Belinda thought, time would tell.

For the next five minutes Belinda sat still whilst Dr. Robbins observed her. He had started to move from one foot to the other as if he was in some sort of trance, and his rhythm was quietly picking up. He started to hum softly to himself and it seemed to Belinda that he was at peace with the world. All that was rudely interrupted as the door to his personal assistants room suddenly opened. In walked Helga with another stack of papers in her hands. Once again she set them down and nodded at Dr. Robbins.

'Dit zijn de Steele Pots and Pans contracten voor het ondertekenen, Dr Robbins.' She said to him. Robbins immediately stopped swaying and humming and said,

'Dank u Helga! Now come and meet Ms. Blumenthal properly!'

Helga calmly looked the naked Belinda up and down and smiled, removed her spectacles and kissed Belinda hard on the mouth. Belinda was stunned for the third time that afternoon, and made a gargled reply as her mouth was now full of Helga's tongue. Helga wasn't put off, perhaps because Robbins was looking on very intently, and stretched her right hand out to gently feel Belinda's right breast. Belinda immediately moaned and saw Robbins out of the corner of her eye start to move from one foot to the other again. Belinda suddenly understood what was going on... Robbins was a voyeur, he needed a show and that was exactly what she and the unsuspecting Helga were going to give him.

Chapter 4;

Helga turns it on;

Belinda moaned a little louder and as she did so, Dr Robbins hummed a little louder, were they in unison Belinda thought. Helga had now caught Belinda's left breast and was passionately teasing the nipple, it started to respond and grew in size with the woman's clumsy touch. Belinda concentrated on removing Helga's woollen jumper. Luckily it had buttons down the front which Belinda quickly undid. She then pulled it off and concentrated on the woollen shirt, again the buttons were easily taken care of and underneath, Helga was naked, no bra or vest to bother with. This is so easy thought Belinda who immediately took hold of Helga's worn tits and started to apply a gentle but firm pressure to them. Helga in her turn started to moan and her hands started to roam down to Belinda's wet vagina. Helga stopped kissing Belinda and moved her tongue to Belinda's now very swollen nipples.

Helga started to nibble Belinda's left nipple with her teeth while licking the rest of her breast with her open mouth. Her hand had now found Belinda's clitoris and was punishing it with two fingers, albeit in a haphazard fashion. Belinda continued to groan and decided to up the game with Helga before she orgasmed. Belinda grabbed Helga's ass and pulled down her linen skirt, it started to rip, but she kept going. It only took a second and the torn skirt was on the floor with Helga's white thong on view for Robbins to see. Belinda couldn't believe that this prissy middle aged woman wore a thong to work. With a practised flick of her hand, Belinda removed the thong and went for Helga's vagina.

Robbins meanwhile had moved across to the desk where Helga had left the contracts and started signing them. He was apparently content with what he had seen, though he did look up constantly to make sure he didn't miss any of the action. By this stage Helga and Belinda were fully enjoying themselves and Belinda had stretched out on the desk with Helga beside her. Both women were masturbating the other and were steadily opening each other's legs wider and wider as they felt their respective orgasms grow.

Helga's big angular tits swung violently in the dying sunlight as she started to swoon and her eyes rolled into the back of her head. She orgasmed loudly as if she had been released from years of tension and Belinda smiled to herself. She at last let her own orgasm surface and attempted to make at least as much noise. On the side lines Dr Robbins clapped the performance and after a suitable period of recovery time for the females, asked Helga to take away the signed contracts and return with a bound copy for each company.

Helga groggily lowered herself off the desk and picked up the pile of papers. She exited the room completely naked pushing back her hair with the odd tear seeping from her eyes still trying to compose herself after her deep orgasm. Belinda sat up with her tits falling gracefully to their normal positions, she was still sitting on the hot desk and asked Dr Robbins if the paperwork was all in order.

'Yes dear Belinda, the deal is done, the legal details have been authorised and we can get on with our work.' Belinda smiled and used her right forefinger to pick up some of Helga's juices from her thighs. 'If I might be so bold,' interjected Dr. Robbins, 'but might I have a taste of that divine liquid?'

'Why yes of course, Dr, how silly of me not to share, here lick my finger....'

Dr. Robbins came across and stuck out his tongue like a five year old, Belinda carefully rolled her finger across it, depositing as much of Helga's and no doubt her own, juices as possible. He slowly licked her finger and asked for more. Belinda obliged him, this time putting two of her fingers into her vaginal slit so that she could obtain the maximum amount of liquid juice as possible. The good Dr. guzzled and smacked his lips in delight, 'Could I be permitted to drink from that wonderful fountain Belinda?' he quietly asked.

Belinda smiled, so he was human, just very, very shy.

'Absolutely.' she replied, swivelling on her ass across the desk to face him whilst opening her legs as wide as possible to accommodate his face and tongue. Dr. Robbins leant forward and started to suck from Belinda's vagina. Belinda knew she would be dry in a few seconds if she didn't take some measures to make herself wet again. Carefully so as not to upset the happily sucking Dr. Robbins Belinda massaged her clitoris with one slim finger and soon had the effect she needed. More juices emanated from her vagina and Robbins sucked more greedily and noisily. After two or three minutes, the naked Helga entered the room with the bound paperwork. She set it down noiselessly and looked questioningly at Belinda. Even though Helga had little English, Belinda knew what she was silently asking,

'What the fuck is going on?'

Belinda held her free hand up in an open palm gesture which clearly said, 'I wish I knew?'

After another ten minutes of sucking, orgasming, clit and breast rubbing, Dr. Robbins decided he had had his fill. He straightened up, adjusted his tweed jacket and said in Dutch,

'Excuse me I need to visit the toilet so please amuse Belinda, Helga, whilst I am gone.'

Belinda was in the dark, and as Robbins left the room she could see Helga smiling at her. Helga immediately went to a drawer in the desk and took out a pen and paper. She quickly wrote down her name, address and phone number and put it in Belinda's jacket which was still strewn across the floor.

'Contact me any time, for business information and personal reasons.'

With that she started to massage Belinda's body and didn't stop until Dr. Robbins returned.

'A very successful afternoon's discussion Belinda and I hope our two companies can build on this very promising start to our business relationship. I for one am already looking forward to our next meeting, as I am sure Helga is.' Dr. Robbins winked at Belinda, licked his lips and showed her to the door.

'Go up to the next floor for your meeting with Mr. Rouse.' and with that he disappeared back into his office.

Chapter 5;

Goedenavond Peter!

Belinda exited the lift and looked for reception. It was empty, perhaps they'd all gone home. Belinda looked at the clock above the small reception desk, it showed 5.30pm. 'At least I'm on time,' she thought. Belinda sat down on a comfortable settee and waited. She knew Peter was aware of her presence in the building, perhaps he was giving her a few much needed moments to put her meeting with Dr Robbins out of her head.

A door opened on the far side of the room and the blonde Cristina walked out of it. She beckoned to Belinda to follow her. The doorway lead to a conference room with a large oval table in its centre, around it were twenty chairs, all in the same dark mahogany wood but the room was empty.

'We don't have time Belinda, but, let's use this table for a 'meeting' sometime in the future.' Cristina kept walking and opened a door on the other side of the conference room. Belinda followed her through to a lobby with thick carpet and well-proportioned leather chairs randomly scattered around. It reminded her of a smoking room in one of the London clubs Tony had taken her to for lunch, during the first week of her induction. Cristina turned to her and erotically fondled Belinda's breasts; she then pushed a button on the wall and reluctantly returned to the conference room blowing a kiss at Belinda as she closed the door.

'My,' Belinda thought, 'how things have changed, she's now chasing me.'

One minute later Peter Rouse appeared at another door and said,

'My darling Belinda, you have survived the rigors of Doctor Pieter Robbins!'

'Peter, how good to see you so soon again. I must say you do look in great shape!'

Rouse walked over to Belinda and kissed her hand.

'Let's move through to what I like to call my pad, Belinda, where I can get a better view of you.'

Rouse turned and led the now slightly panting Belinda by the hand into the next room. Belinda gasped as she entered. To use the word stunning was an under-statement, the old warehouse roof had been replaced by a beautiful atrium and whilst the building's walls on the canal side were still built of brick with their traditional windows, the other side had been replaced with massive sheets of glass. It had been elegantly constructed, and the area contained everything one needed to live in one open space. Kitchen, lounge, bathrooms and bedrooms were all on show with only glass divisions. Nudity was not seemingly a modest option in this living space.

Peter caressed her breast and ran his other hand down her spine, feeling the shape of her pert ass with his palm. Belinda breathed deeply and quickly dispelled the thoughts of Cristina from her mind. She breathed deeply a second time, she couldn't help it, this man had some sort of deep sexual attraction for her and she found herself happily relinquishing her will to his touch. Rouse kissed her, and undid her jacket. Belinda could feel his penis hardening as he moved even closer to her thighs. He gently pulled her blouse up over her breasts mentally thanking her for her lack of bra and began to massage the exposed bare flesh. Belinda moaned deeply and fumbled for Peters cock.

Peter pushed Belinda onto the kitchen sink and started to fondle her tits. She opened her legs wide and Peter positioned his mouth over her clitoris. His tongue went to work and Belinda relaxed against the taps in its certainty of delivering her pleasure. She slowly removed Peter's clothing, his body scent aroused her further and she kissed his hand. Peter responded by leaving her clitoris and moving his mouth to hers. Their tongues entwined, she tasted her vaginal fluid and moved her mouth down to his penis. She took him completely into her mouth, tasting the flesh of mankind. Up and down she went, taking him deeper with each cycle. His hard penis had now reached the back of her throat, and she timed her breathing to stop herself from gagging. Then it was all over, Peter came and Belinda sucked up the hot frothy white liquid semen. She adored the salt, and it saved her from having to eat too many high protein peanuts. She smiled at this ridiculous thought which had just come to her that very moment when her mind should have been focused on other more important things.

Peter massaged her neck, 'What are you smiling at Belinda?'

'A really silly thought,' she replied, 'but if you must know it was about salt.'

'Ha ha, not pots and pans then, so you're human after all!' they both laughed happy in each other's embrace.

'But enough of this foreplay, I want to fuck you hard now Belinda, what position shall we take?

Belinda thought for a moment and said, 'Well, if you want a deeply penetrating experience then why not the aptly named Leg Glider.'

'Why yes of course,' replied Peter, 'lie down on the bed and raise your right leg.'

Belinda did as she was told making sure she supported her head with her bent left arm. Peter knelt beside her and placed her raised leg on his shoulder. He slowly entered her and kept going. Belinda moaned deeply for what seemed the fiftieth time that day, the angle of penetration was superb as his penis touched her clit with every movement. Peter took his breath in even spasms as he went in and out, penetrating her cervix deeper each and every time. They both reached orgasm level far too quickly for their liking and the bed became a sea of body fluids. However they had managed to keep their rhythm for at least five minutes before collapsing on their backs exhausted. Peter was the first to stir and got up to check his watch.

'I have dinner organised for 8.00pm at one of my special restaurants, which I hope you will enjoy, then a trip to the casino to test out your luck.'

Peter quickly changed into a dark pants and roll neck combination which was both casual and smart. This was essential as it would also allow him access to the casino later that evening. Belinda opened her briefcase and quickly pulled out her crumpled, skimpy and extremely revealing evening gown.

'Wow!' said Peter, 'what else have you got in there?'

Belinda Blinked.

They left by private elevator which lead to the garage underneath the building where Peter kept his black Porsche 911 Gembella Avalanche. They jumped into the extremely low slung vehicle, Belinda's gown slipped revealing her attributes and Peter quickly drove them to the restaurant taking the opportunity to show

Belinda the major sights of Amsterdam at night. He eventually pulled up outside a chic little place called Restaurant d'Albert, tossed the key at the valet and they disappeared inside.

Belinda looked around for the first time whilst pulling her non-existent gown back into place after the ravages of the car journey and saw that the small intimate restaurant was themed in the era of the 1920's just after the First World War. Beautiful chandeliers hung from the ceilings, gas lamps spluttered giving a timeless ambience to the dining area and the waiters were all dressed in dinner jackets with tails. The floor and panelling was all polished oak, reminiscent of Peter's head office, probably one of the reasons he liked dining here.

Menus were given out and Belinda's heart jumped when she saw the prices of the starters.

'An aperitif I believe would be in order, Belinda.' said Peter, 'what do you fancy whilst we peruse the menu?'

'Thank you Peter, I'll have the Campari if you don't mind.'

'Excellent choice, I'll join you in that,

They eventually ordered fish starters with steak for their main course. The restaurant was French in food style and the garlic was heavy, but the food was out of this world. Belinda had eaten many a fine meal but this one was exceptional. Of course no good meal was perfect unless it had the correct wine, and the wine waiter was very attentive to their table. Belinda had a shrewd idea why this was so, her skimpy dress had decided to stabilise itself just below her nipples and for that she was thankful. Peter seemed happy, he had talked over dinner about his business, his expansion plans, how Belinda's company could grow with them and how he wanted to introduce Belinda to his wife Cris. He called them similar in outlook, and Belinda wondered what he meant. Did she wear virtually nothing when they went out to dinner, or was that just the lot of the supplier? No doubt time would tell. The name Cris also rang a bell, but she just couldn't place it.

Soon it was nearly time to move onto the casino and the two bottles of Margaux drunken during the meal had left Belinda feeling a little tipsy. Her drunken state had further increased when they shared a decent bottle of vintage port which Belinda felt ended the meal on a very special high. As she got up to leave the alcohol took hold of her and she stumbled on her right high heel, lost her balance and fell over, the vintage port was obviously having its desired effect. The dress was immediately pulled away from her breasts and at the same time came riding up her thighs to end up in a ball around her stomach. She was now virtually naked apart from her sexy high heels. A sound of clapping and the odd whistle came from the few other remaining diners as they watched this impromptu performance. Belinda raised herself to her knees with her tits flopping all over the place and promptly removed her heels. She then slipped the dress off over her head and wrapped the heels in it. Completely naked she turned to Peter and said, 'I knew this garment, hic, would come in useful for something, hic, it makes a terrific handbag!'

Peter laughed as Belinda curtsied to the cheering restaurant. She belched, cleared her swimming head and walked slowly out of the room waving her tits and swaying her ass seductively at the goggling clientele.

Chapter 6;

Casino Etoile, Amsterdam;

A tipsy Peter and Belinda entered the Casino lobby and half way across they heard a Russian accent shout out, 'Peter… why are you and your female friend ignoring me, come and greet my personal assistant, you know she likes you very much…'

Peter turned round, smiled and said, 'Allow me to introduce my English friend Miss Belinda Blumenthal. Belinda, meet Grigor Calanski and his assistant Lara. By the way, this gentleman is the biggest supplier of quality Russian vodka and caviar to my organisation.'

The extremely bear like Grigor Calanski moved ponderously to his feet, stubbed out his cigar and kissed Belinda's proffered hand. She recoiled at the grease left by his lips, but regained her composure almost immediately thinking, 'A Russian entrepreneur… hmmm, surely he has a need for pots and pans, Russia is a big place. Thank goodness I'm in a Casino, surely my luck is well and truly in this night.'

'English, meet Lara my so to speak right hand man, Peter, come and join us for a drink!'

Belinda and Peter walked over to their table, Belinda sat down opposite Grigor and crossed her long legs. She was going to make sure her body language said what she couldn't.

'You look so delightful English,' the Russian said, 'you suit black, and your breasts stick out so nicely, better than Lara's.

He laughed and looked at both women with a derisory sneer.

Lara quickly interjected in perfect English but with a heavy Russian accent, 'He's a Russian slob and the sooner you turn around and walk out of this Casino the better it will be for you!'

Grigor hastily added, 'Now, now, now Lara don't be too hasty, Peter has told me this is no ordinary girl, she demands respect, she's a Sales Director, and we need them to further our business goals, don't we Lara?'

Grigor looked directly at Lara and she nodded hesitantly, saying,

'Yes we do, even if they are English, beautiful but stupid.'

'Now that's settled, please join us for a session at the tables, Lara and I would love to get to know you better.'

Belinda smiled at Peter and said, 'Yes I will, no doubt it will be very enlightening!'

'That is good.' Grigor snapped his fingers and ordered four dry Martini's.

'I understand you represent one of the market leaders in cooking implements, do you have any representation in Russia or its Confederacies?'

Belinda shook her head and said, 'It's a geographic region we've been considering, but because of its fragmentation we've been unable to appoint a suitable distributor, or trust a major sales outlet.'

'Good answer English, because you have not met me, that is, until tonight... I would like to do business with you, and I think it could be very profitable for us both.'

Belinda turned her legs toward Grigor, she instinctively uncrossed them whilst at the same time, very slowly, opened them slightly. The split in her evening gown fell between her legs revealing her upper thighs. Grigor coughed and Belinda knew she had him on the hook, all she had to do was to reel him in, and she had the rest of the evening to do that. But what should she do about Lara, that was the question, how could she make her a friend and not an enemy. Belinda was too savvy to realise she couldn't bypass her, she was obviously the guardian of the gate, but perhaps she could use Peter to achieve her ends with Grigor. What the hell, it was worth a try, and Belinda started to put her thoughts into action.

Peter turned to Belinda and whispered,

'You may have now gathered that I am very keen on sexual fantasies, and that my aim is to make any woman I want my own.'

Belinda nodded, unsure where this whispered conversation was going to lead and thought of Peter's prowess at falling deeply asleep at the Horse and Jockey.

Unfortunately my plans for you tonight have changed because of Grigors unannounced visit. You see, Lara is with him, which rarely ever happens, I need to seduce her, make her one of my favourites and reluctantly leave your needs until another time.'

Belinda held back a satisfied smile. She now had the perfect opportunity to get Lara out of her hair whilst sucking Grigor in and with him access to the continent of Russia and its millions of customers.

'Peter, I'm disappointed, but I do understand, perhaps you could help me by letting Lara know that I gave way for her, and that I respect her very much.'

Peter smiled pleased he had got his way so easily, 'You are a devious lady Belinda, I can see I am going to have to watch you very carefully in the future!'

Peter kissed Belinda on her right hand and immediately took Lara across the room to the Craps table.

Now free, Belinda wandered across to the Black Jack tables, at that moment Grigor came up behind her and casually brushed her ass with his hand, feeling for any hint of underwear.

'You like this bareback riding I see English.'

Belinda nodded, 'Yes, it's much more exciting than betting, don't you think?'

Grigor laughed and threw some chips onto the table.

'First things first, English, first things first, now sit on my lap and let's see if we can beat the House.'

It was obvious that the Russian was a practised gambler, and after an hour of success Grigor scooped up his winnings and threw them into Belinda's lap. She caught them deftly with her evening dress, showing an indecently large area of thigh in the process.

'Well caught English, now let's cash them in and see some more of those wonderful legs with a glass of champagne tucked between them!'

Grigor and Belinda strolled out of the Casino, and turned immediately right down a somewhat seedy street in the very centre of Amsterdam's famous red light district. All the shop windows had semi naked girls parading their wares in a two metre garishly lit space with pulsating neon tubes of coloured light. Heavy vibe music pelted out of the shop entrances, each one competing with the other for the few customers left on the street at this late hour. A smell of weed hung in the stale night time air, as Grigor guided her down a semi-lit alleyway roughly fondling her ass and touching her vaginal lids as they walked. About three houses along they went up a couple of steps and Grigor pushed the intercom. It was quickly answered. Grigor whispered the words, 'My Auntie is sick.'

A voice replied, 'What is wrong with her?'

Grigor grunted, rolled his eyes and said, 'She has Harpes.'

Belinda grimaced, hoping it wasn't a family trait.

A tall blonde man opened the door and recognised Grigor immediately.

'Grigor Calanski, by the Norse Gods, what's kept you, we thought you were going to stand us up!'

'My friend, I was on business development, and look what I have brought with me!'

The blonde guy ushered them in without saying a word.

'Zara has been waiting for you, and she's not happy Calanski, you've fucked up big this time!'

'Don't worry you know I can handle Zara, besides she'll adore meeting Ms. Blumenthal. Now take us to my table, prepare two bottles of champagne, two servings of Black Sea Caviar... the best mind you, and a dozen salted oysters... quick!'

The blonde ushered them down a flight of steps into a large room with about ten tables in it. He quickly showed them to one in the corner and disappeared to place Grigors order.

'Who is Zara... she seems quite intimidating?' said Belinda slowly looking around.

Grigor looked across the room and replied, 'I think you are about to find out!'

Chapter 7;

The Countess Zara;

A middle aged woman dressed in a long white evening dress entered the room and made straight for the Calanski table. She was a stunningly beautiful woman who wore little make up, her high cheek bones and sharp features reminded Belinda of the Russian ballerinas she had worshiped as a child. Her breasts were magnificent and even Belinda could see her thighs were every man's dream… long, powerful and smooth.

'So, you thought you would keep me waiting Mr Calanski.'

'I think you'll find the wait worthwhile, can I introduce my new business associate Belinda Blumenthal… English, this is the Countess Zara of Leningrad our host tonight.'

'Why I'm delighted to meet you Countess.' Belinda replied.

'Darling, enchanted, I hope you are keeping my little Grigor here on the path to fame and riches, after all he knows how to spend the money he does so well at making.'

As if to emphasise her point the waiter arrived with the two bottles of champagne, caviar and oysters.

'A celebration I see.' said the Countess.

Grigor smiled and opened his arms, 'Please join us Countess Zara, I presume you've been too busy to eat tonight.'

'Thank you I will, business is booming and I'm short staffed again, my Russian girls just can't keep up with my clients and the Dutch girls do so know their European working rights. It's a nightmare!'

Grigor laughed, 'Such is the way of business Countess, feast or famine!'

Suddenly the lights dimmed and the tall blonde man appeared on a little stage discretely tucked away from general view.

'Tonight I give you our final act, our resident singer and Parisian strip tease artiste, Chantelle!'

A polite applause from the surrounding tables saw a mostly naked female take the stage. Her breasts were covered in delicate muslin which enhanced her mystique, but left nothing to the imagination. A small dental floss thong failed to partially cover her lower parts and black long leather boots completed her outfit. The most striking thing about the girl was her perfectly shaven head, it was so beautiful Belinda had to look twice. Gleaming with oil, the sheer nakedness of this part of her body demanded attention and it was only when she started to sing that the audience started to appreciate the rest of her sensual body.

The Countess slowly got up making sure not to disturb the act going on in front of them. She whispered to Grigor

'I'll see you in my rooms in ten minutes, bring Belinda, she looks, let me say... interesting.'

Grigor nodded and kept his eyes fixed on Chantelle who was by now singing her second number, one of his favourites, a sexy version of, 'A walk in the black forest.' Belinda could see Grigor was enjoying it and whilst she knew the tune she couldn't place the words as they were in French. Chantelle was now completely naked except for her black boots. Once Zara was out of earshot Calanski turned to Belinda and said very softly,

'Whatever you encounter in the next two hundred minutes react with complete acceptance, remember I have your back, you are my guest and my future business partner, I will not let you come to any harm. I repeat, I will not let you come to any harm!'

Belinda blinked;

'What the hell is going on,' she thought, 'is this Russian Mafia, or just one of those great evenings out where crazy things happen?'

She nodded her acceptance. Grigor got up and motioned Belinda to follow him. They slipped behind a satin curtain near their table, Grigor momentarily stopped and went back to retrieve the newly opened bottle of champagne and hurried up a set of steep stairs to the upper floor. Belinda followed him, eager to find out what was behind all the mystery.

They entered a small antechamber, Grigor knocked on the only door leading off it and waited, seconds later a completely naked Zara appeared and motioned them into her private rooms.

'Please make yourselves feel at home, and Belinda, no clothes.'

Belinda watched Grigor undress, it was the first time she had the opportunity to do so, he was big, but he had the stance of an athlete, perhaps a past shot putter or more likely a javelin thrower, accurate and deadly. She remembered Grigors last words and slipped her evening dress off. Belinda felt good and she was definitely up for anything the Russians could throw at her.

'Sit down beside me Belinda.' Zara pointed to the large, round leather settee which filled the centre of the room.

'Grigor attend my other side.' They both did as requested and Zara started to touch Belinda with one hand and Grigor with the other.

'How beautiful you both are.' she murmured still speaking in English.

'Of course Grigor is a regular visitor, but you Belinda, you are a newcomer. Do you wish to visit me each time you visit Amsterdam?'

Belinda nodded, she could do nothing else as Zara's hand was now expertly massaging her clitoris, and she was concentrating on not responding in any negative way. Grigor had a similar problem as Zara had moved onto his penis and was now ensuring it was responding in the proper way a Russian male should.

'Touch me Belinda, touch me Grigor.' Belinda looked across at Grigor and followed his lead, he was clumsily poking Zara's right breast. Belinda started to stroke her left breast and after a few seconds moved onto her nipple. It hardened quickly and Belinda bent to suck it. Zara groaned softly, Belinda intensified the pace with the use of her tongue and at the same time sent her hand down to the top of the Countess's thighs. She was semi shaven and the remaining lightly coloured pubic hairs proved to be the signpost to her labia. Belinda quickly started to slowly pull apart her lids and began stimulating her clitoris.

Grigor too was not slouching as he had placed his other hand around Zara's back and was searching for her asshole with his fingers whilst continuing to massage her breast. The Countess's groans became deeper as she succumbed to the inevitable climax. It was amazing that she still kept her hands active on Belinda and Grigor whilst she experienced her first orgasm of the session. But the intensity of the situation was too much even for a Madame of her quality and she soon fell back onto the leather sofa.

'Fuck me Grigor, Belinda, come down on me and give me my feast.' Zara moved herself onto the centre of the settee and her acolytes did as they were instructed. Grigor opened her legs wide and entered her, penetrating deeply to ensure she felt no tardiness in his actions. He quickly picked up his rhythm and started to powerfully fuck her. Meanwhile Belinda had gotten into a squat position over Zara's face and gently came down on her, carefully maintaining her balance so as not to fall on top of her and so break the erotic spell. Belinda's vagina had opened wide in the squat position so it was simple for the Countess to start penetrating her with her tongue. It only took two seconds for her clitoris to start singing and very soon Belinda had to concentrate on not giving the Countess an early shower.

The Countess soon realised Belinda was not a true professional at this type of work and put her hands under Belinda's ass to ensure her stability. Zara kept licking and soon Belinda's juices started to run clear. Belinda started to orgasm and the Countess picked up the pace, Grigor too realised what was going on and he started to thrust harder and longer. Zara couldn't keep up her work rate and succumbed to a shuddering orgasm which saw her lose control of Belinda's clit. It was time for Belinda to back up and she did so instinctively, Grigor too pulled out leaving the Countess panting heavily as she came to terms with the massive orgasm she had just experienced.

At last she regained her composure and quickly clapped her hands, twice. Immediately a series of hidden spotlights flashed on.

Belinda Blinked;

The lights illuminated a huge crowd gathered outside the building. Belinda realised she was in the middle of a huge shop window. What looked like hundreds of excited tourists were enjoying the spectacle and just as suddenly the lights dimmed and the tallish blonde man entered the room.

'Countess, 269.' was all he said as he bowed and reversed out of the room.

'Well done English,' Grigor growled, 'you have performed admirably, and broken our record.'

Grigor flipped Belinda onto the settee ready to penetrate her whilst the Countess prepared herself to go down on her. Belinda opened her legs wide to accept Grigor and placed her hands under the ass of the Countess. Then it all started again, Belinda had been in many an odd encounter, but never with two Russians quite like this.

Grigor thrusted, Belinda licked and the Countess concentrated on not falling on Belinda. It was a battle that the middle aged woman, fit as she was, was never going to win. Belinda's accurate tongue probing soon set Zara orgasming. Grigor unfortunately wasn't having as much luck with Belinda's vagina. So what was a business girl to do but to tighten her muscles, it soon had the desired effect and Grigor started to come. Belinda finished the threesome off with a faked orgasm which entailed a lot of shouted expletives, many of which the Russians had never heard before. Finally they all fell apart and recovered in their own time.

'What record did I break Grigor?' asked Belinda.

'English, you are so competitive, we have just made wonderful love and you ask me about records, surely you should be thinking of humming birds and beautiful cherubs floating on soft clouds?'

'Grigor, don't fuck with me, don't give me partial information and expect me to ignore it. Besides, I am competitive, it's who I am, it's what I do and it's how I succeed. So tell me, what record?'

Grigor laughed again, 'You forgot to mention persistence English, but yes, we are all impressed. The record you see was for the biggest crowd of people you attracted, 269.'

Belinda smiled and said, 'So what was the previous crowd number?'

'You don't give up do you English, 233 people, but over a longer period and the weather was better.'

Belinda lay back and sipped her champagne happy in the knowledge that she was a winner, even in this most unusual of competitions.

Chapter 8;
Amsterdam to London sky high;

At the airport Belinda hoped she would have enough time to replace her missing thong, bra and her somewhat tired but still sexy heels so that she could feel slightly more respectable for the London flight. Belinda always thought that smart footwear was an important factor when meeting someone for the first time. She didn't intend to meet anyone, just to look respectable enough to get through security and on the plane. She was out of luck, all the clothing concessions at Amsterdam airport had closed by the time Peter had dropped her off. There was nothing for it except to stick it out.

Belinda went through security without being strip searched and entered the departure lounge. The noise of many females chatting excitedly wafted across the large area, she looked around trying to ascertain where the noise was coming from. Then she saw them, about thirty ladies were standing around in small groups waiting for the flight to London. Even stranger they were all sloppily dressed in crumpled business attire similar to herself. Belinda went over to them wondering what was going on, were they Dutch, they certainly dressed like they were...

'Hello,' said one of the ladies in English as she approached them, 'the way you're dressed you must be on our flight as well? That's great; I think that makes thirty one of us!'

Belinda smiled and thought, 'this seems to be genuine, what on earth is going on?'

Belinda listened to the chit chat trying to pick up any clue as to why these trampishly dressed women were here.

'Yes my sales have been shooting up with the new TV advert, have you noticed an increase?' The question wasn't directed at Belinda but at the lady standing next to her.

'Why yes, my plastic ware has been especially popular, I just wish we could get a good supplier of pots and pans on board... so many customers keep asking for a quality pot.'

Belinda's ears pricked up immediately, pots and pans... it suddenly dawned on her. They must be attending a big weekend national sales conference in London at the O2. Tony had briefly mentioned it to her and was a bit miffed Steele's hadn't been invited to speak.

'Sorry,' Belinda said, 'I don't mean to mislead you, but I'm a supplier, I just happen to be dressed similarly.'

'Goodness!' the first lady exclaimed, 'so you're not on the official pre conference Dutch fact finding tour?'

The second lady said, 'Who are you with?'

'Steele's Pots and Pans.' replied Belinda still struggling with the company name.

'Crikey,' the first lady said, 'quality stuff then.'

'We like to think so... what's your names?'

'I'm Betty Wilkes and this is our acting area manager Vicky Woods.'

'Belinda Blumenthal, very nice to meet you... can I get you both a cup of tea?'

'Seeing as you're the supplier we'd prefer a glass of Chardonnay...
you know, help settle our nerves for the flight and all that!' said a
smiling Vicky.

'Ladies after my own heart!' replied a smiling Belinda. Ten minutes
later saw the three of them sipping their Chardonnay as the aircraft
started loading.

'So you wouldn't mind popping into the conference next weekend,
we'd only want a ten minute presentation, and we'd love having
your gear on board.' said Vicky.

'Be delighted.' said Belinda hardly believing her luck. It turned out
the ladies both worked for a direct retail door to door and coffee
morning's organisation. Whilst they weren't big at present they
were strong in the north and southeast of England. More
importantly they were growing steadily and that sort of business
would never affect the big retailers who Belinda presently relied on.

Vicky made a quick call to their central administration and spoke to
one of the conference organisers. They were over the moon with
the idea as they had had a few people pull out at the last minute
and Steele's the manufacturer would be a big attraction.

'You're on Belinda... mines a gin and tonic when we get seated!'

'My pleasure Vicky, and thanks Betty!'

Belinda was in the final row of the plane and was allowed to board
from the rear steps. Once they'd taken off she organised the drinks

for Betty and Vicky. What fun she thought as she started to prepare some notes for her future presentation!

The plane wasn't overly full and scattered around, mostly at the back, were uniformed air crew changing locations for morning flights. A smart looking leggy blonde with decent looking breasts in co-pilot uniform was sat across the aisle from Belinda. After ten minutes of flying she asked Belinda, purely out of curiosity, why all the ladies were wearing such sloppy business attire.

'It's a domestic utensil trade trip returning from Holland and believe it or not the sloppy business attire is their uniform.' Belinda replied.

'How very interesting, and what a most unusual form of dress... my names Hazel by the way.'

'Belinda... come and sit next to me!'

Hazel changed seats and settled herself down beside Belinda.

'Hot in here,' said Belinda as she opened the top button of her blouse showing a fair amount of cleavage.

'Here,' said Hazel, 'I'm a co-pilot and I understand these things, let me adjust your air vent... it's just above you.'

Hazel's long arm snaked upwards and twisted the nozzle letting a stream of cooling air flow over Belinda's face and tits.

'How efficient of you Hazel, are you always so responsive?'

'Why Belinda, I believe I am... at least all my best friends say so.'

Hazel started to move her fitted, tight skirt up her thighs and Belinda unbuttoned a lower section of the blouse. A change in the note of the engine prompted Hazel to say,

'We're half way back, the planes starting to descend, rub my clit Belinda... please.'

Belinda obliged Hazel and Hazel obliged Belinda. By the time the landing gear was down the girls had become firm friends and were on the brink of orgasm. With their seat belts fastened they were ready for the bumpy landing in the windy conditions. As the plane's tyres screeched multiple times on contact with the tarmac both girls climaxed simultaneously. It was as well their screams were muffled by the landing, Belinda didn't need any adverse publicity in front of her thirty new customers.

'Tough landing Belinda!' purred Hazel, 'but everything worked out very well I thought, even the aerofoil flaps came up at the correct time.'

Hazel laughed and straightened her skirt; now in back to work mode. Belinda buttoned up her blouse and put on her tired but still sexy high heels, yes it was a very eventful flight.

Chapter 9;

Motivating the Salesforce;

Belinda walked into head office. She wanted to personally deliver the freshly signed contracts with Rouse's company but it was now 5.30 pm and the place was fairly empty with most activity coming from the cleaning staff. She walked into her office, threw the briefcase onto the desk, removed her jacket and high heels and slumped into her chair. Someone coughed and Belinda looked up. It was Des Martin her Regional Sales Manager for London and the South East.

'What the fuck is he doing here,' she thought. Belinda smiled,

'Hi Des, what's up?'

'Hi Belinda, I'm afraid I've got some bad news.'

'You've not smashed your bloody car up have you?' Belinda quickly replied.

'No... it, it's not as bad as that.'

Belinda heaved a sigh of relief, Tony always got mad when she had to report a written off car to him.

'Well don't just stand there man, come on, spit it out!'

'I'm afraid, I'm... I'm going to resign.'

'What do you mean resign Des... you're my second best performing manager... you don't need to resign!'

'Yes Belinda, you're correct, but my wife has walked out and I don't know what to do... I'm devastated.'

'Des, life is shit, but we all move on, I remember when my pet parrot died... but I got over it!'

'Belinda, don't compare my wife to a dead parrot... she was perfect... well, her nose was a bit big, but it wasn't a beak!'

'Des, what do you mean perfect?'

'She had great tits... nearly as good as yours, and that's why I'm resigning, I can't keep looking at yours knowing I can't touch my wife's... it's killing me!

Belinda rolled her eyes, she'd only been in the country one hour and here she was, getting the old tits out once again to save the company's ass.

'Des, if it helps you, just feel mine, they're probably not as good, but what the hell, give them a good licking.'

Des stood up and walked around the desk. He stood behind Belinda and put his arms over her shoulders. He gently touched the silken fabric, undid the four buttons and slid his warm hands over her breasts. He found her nipples and started to rub them. Belinda groaned for the sixtieth time in two days. Des gently removed Belinda's blouse and noted she wasn't wearing a brassiere.... again. He slowly pulled her long luxurious black hair up over her face, bent his head down over her swan like neck and slurped at her tits.

'God, Belinda, they taste as good as they look.' murmured Des.

'Oh that's good,' replied Belinda, 'I do try to use a quality skin moistener each night before bed, it's obviously having the desired effect.'

Des moaned, his puckered lips latched onto Belinda's fast extending nipples. Foaming saliva from his mouth started to drip down Belinda's body, it slowly gathered in the well of her beautifully formed tummy button. Des continued his sloppy enjoyment of Belinda's tits until she had had enough. How did she tell him she was getting bored, would it send him over the top? Could she risk it? She certainly didn't want to change a sopping wet skirt at the office.

Belinda gently took Des's face in her hands and lifted it off her breasts saying,

'Now… now, you've had enough Des, best get yourself off home and think of what we could be doing next week.'

Des emitted a deep sigh and said,

'Thanks Belinda, you know I'd do anything for you.' and with a quick sob he left Belinda's office.

Belinda put her blouse, high heels and jacket back on as Des went home to his empty life. He hadn't resigned. Belinda hadn't needed to recruit a new manager and she'd made big inroads into her first relationship with a key member of her sales staff. She felt he was now motivated, reinvigorated and up for the job with her unorthodox intervention, he had left satisfied, if sad, but wanting more.

Ten minutes later a composed Belinda knocked on Tony's door not really expecting him to be in.

'Enter.' was the gruff reply.

Belinda walked in, sat down and flung her slightly damp hair over her shoulders.

'Boy could I do with a gin and tonic.' she said.

Tony looked up from the massive computer printout he was studying and smiled.

'Yes it's the time! Friday afternoon and all that, but tell me how did Amsterdam go?'

'It went perfectly to plan Tony and with potentially a big bonus for the company!'

Intrigued Tony spoke into his intercom, 'Giselle, come and join us.' He got up and started to prepare three gin and tonics. Giselle glided into the room very much back to her old self and sporting an extremely modern haircut.

'Wow, I like the hair Giselle.' said Belinda.

'Thank you Belinda, I decided to have a change of style... after our long talk!'

'Come on Belinda tell us about your Amsterdam bonus.' said Tony passing around the drinks.

'Well I tied up the contracts with Rouse's purchasing director and then went out to dinner with Peter. The rest is all a bit vague, but during the evening I met his Russian supplier called Grigor Calanski and he wants to do business with us. Seemingly Peter has been singing our praises and Calanski is very interested.'

'Is that the whole story Belinda?' Giselle said with a note of suspicion in her voice.

'Giselle, would I keep anything from you and Tony?'

Giselle laughed and said, 'Yes you would!'

'Promise I'll tell you another time, but the Dutch contract is solid.'

Tony and Giselle looked at each other, smiled and nodded. Giselle got up and made another round of G and T's.

Tony said, 'Looks like more detective work for you to do Giselle, it's a fine thing when my Sales Director only talks to my PA and leaves me, the Boss, out of it all.'

'Poor Tony, you wouldn't enjoy the sordid details of my job, but all I can say is that Calanski is successful and well connected. He's in London in ten days' time so we'll talk turkey then, and Tony, he wants to meet you, so make the evening available.'

Tony looked sideways at Belinda and winked. She laughed and left the room knowing Tony was well pleased.

In her office she rang Bella at reception. There was no reply so she rang her cell.

'Hi, Belinda, Bella here, what do you need?'

'Where are you? I'm thinking of a drink at the Pentra with perhaps Giselle.'

'Sounds good, I'm just in M&S getting a few items for our lunch tomorrow, be done in five, so I'll meet you there in twenty. Ciao.'

Bella hung up and Belinda rang Giselle.

'Hi Giselle, fancy a few at the Pentra before home time?'

'Phew, thought you'd never ask, yes!'

'What about lover boy?'

'I'm free for two hours at least, he's off to the gym!'

'Great, can you drive as I've had a bit of Chardonnay already today.'

'No problem Belinda, we can get a taxi from the Pentra easily and you can retrieve the Mercedes tomorrow morning.'

Thirty minutes later Giselle, Bella and Belinda found themselves ensconced at the same table where they had so elegantly entertained the Regional Sales Managers only one week ago.

Belinda raised her glass, 'To us!' she toasted. The three glasses chinked and the girls knocked back the Chilean Chardonnay in grand style.

Chapter 10;
Sir James pops up;

Belinda was feeling frustrated, she still hadn't heard about what had happened to Bella at the BBQ.

'Bella, how did you get all that lipstick over you and how did you get on with small cock Stirling?'

'Who?' Bella and Giselle chorused.

'You heard me, small cock Stirling, Jim Bean, you know... the yank, Bella, please back me up on this!'

'Belinda, you need to know that Jim Stirling just used me to research all our products that could be acceptable in the USA that Sunday evening. We had a late dinner around 11pm and then his chauffeur drove me home. He said he was on the early morning flight to Texas and that I should come with you when you visit him next week. He seemed pleased with my work.'

'Bella, I do not believe you.' said Belinda. 'We thought that he'd given you a really rough time as we'd not seen you on the Monday morning.'

'No, he was a thorough gentleman.'

'Good, so it all went well with Stirling after the Tombola, but what did you get up to when I was in the maze and Giselle was in the garage?'

'Ah ha,' replied Bella very quickly, 'now that is a story worth hearing.'

'Spill the beans Bella.' said Giselle.

The girls laughed and replenished their wine glasses.

'Sir James met me at the BBQ and told me Tony had given him responsibility for looking after me that afternoon. Of course I was very flattered, even though he's a bit past what I would have preferred. Anyway as it turned out I needn't have worried about him; he delegated me to one of his horse racing cronies, some Duke or other, called Clarence as I later found out. This guy Clarence took me into the house and started showing me the portraits in the west wing... or perhaps it was the east wing, but no matter, I soon ended up in a bedroom with him.

He stripped me, God knows what he did with my thong... probably ate it the way he was aroused. Then he tied me to a four poster bed with some stupid green plastic handcuffs. I was now star shaped. He then stripped off and boy oh boy, did he look good. You could tell he was in the racing set... well-tanned and hung like a stallion, though to be honest I've never seen one of those... yet!

Belinda and Giselle took the pause in Bella's story to laugh about the handcuffs, the stallion and to pour out more wine.

'Well then he got this red lipstick from somewhere and started painting me with it... he said it reminded him of his days in Rhodesia. I thought to myself, you're just making me look like one of those tarts on the Old Kent Road. I also reckoned he needed glasses as his aim was terrible, I mean he made a horrible job of my lips, took him five goes to get it right. Then he went onto my tits, now even you girls have to admit they're not exactly small, he just couldn't circle around the nipples for love nor money. I felt like doing it for him, only I was all tied up. Next he went lower... and do I mean lower... my toes, first time I've had lipstick on my toes... ever tried it Belinda?'

'Can't say that I have Bella though thinking about it, if it was strawberry flavour, I might give it a go!'

Giselle nodded her head in agreement and they all laughed. They opened the second bottle of Chardonnay and Bella continued.

'So there I was, all painted up and waiting for his next move; but before Clarence could take any action this tall lady dressed in white walked into the room. He hadn't even had the gumption to lock the door he was that excited at getting me into bed. She didn't seem too happy at what was going on because they had a fearful row, and she insisted he release me from my cuffs immediately.

Belinda and Giselle sat mesmerised; they just couldn't comprehend what Bella was telling them, it was so utterly impossible.

'She made him release me and ordered me out of the room, but before I left she started to whip me with a horse crop on the ass. I have to tell you it made me move out of that room pretty fast, clothes or no clothes! She was shouting at him the whole time, but I don't think he got whipped, though I suppose in her eyes he deserved it. I closed the door behind me and that's where I bumped into Sir James. Of course he had a quick fumble with my tits and clit, but he soon had my clothes out of the room and back on me albeit with the help of a few safety pins. Then he lead me through the house and back outside to where the tombola was starting.'

Belinda gasped and said,

'So you met the Duchess and it was her husband Clarence who was preparing you for a fucking?'

'Yup, that's it Belinda.'

'But the Duchess,' burbled Belinda, 'she didn't say a thing to me, though to be honest we did have other matters on our minds... or should I say tongues, no wonder she was so pissed at the world... and that of course is why she bid for me at the tombola... revenge on Clarence and possibly his best pal Godwin!'

Giselle's two hours were now up and as she excused herself the name,

'Belinda!' thundered across the bar.

Belinda bit her lip and Sir James Godwin pushed his way towards their table. She inwardly groaned, this strenuous day was obviously not over. She'd planned going to Bella's place as previously arranged, having a little bit of dinner at the local Beefeater, a naughty movie on Bella's big screen and then blessed sleep. Saturday was for shopping when she'd hoped to purchase her horse riding gear. However that was all now irrelevant, they would have to entertain Sir James and she had a shrewd idea what that would amount to...

Belinda turned to Bella,

'A quick strategy meeting; let's do a Regional Sales Manager stunt for Sir James, let's try and get him well and truly on our side.'

Bella nodded, she knew the score. She got up and went to the toilets.

'Please sit down, please join us,' Belinda said politely.

'So what brings you here this late Friday afternoon Belinda?' said Sir James as he pulled up a heavily tooled leather chair to the table.

'Well sir, I was just debriefing Bella on my successful negotiations with the Peter Rouse supermarket chain in Holland. I just flew back this afternoon, and to be honest, we've done extremely well with them.'

Sir James was obviously flabbergasted, 'Where's Bella?'

'Toilets sir.'

'Hrrmmph, suppose we all need them sometimes,' he muttered, 'Did you meet Rouse's wife Cristina... or Cris as her friends know her?'

Belinda blinked;

The penny dropped... 'Cris, why yes, isn't she in reception?'

Sir James laughed, 'Well Belinda, at least you didn't work that one out... Cristina works partly in reception, but her main job is information flow... to you and me that means spying. She's basically his eyes and ears throughout the operation and she's also my niece.'

Belinda blinked for the second time in two minutes.

'Ahh, Bella, refreshed from the loos I see.' boomed Sir James.

Bella sat down, her wettened breasts rubbing sexily against her blouse. Her supine nipples had not yet been stimulated enough to show, but it was obvious that Sir James' eyes were on high alert.

Belinda got up and excused herself. Sir James changed seats to sit next to Bella. He poured Bella another glass of wine, patted her leg and said, 'Good work last weekend, my pal Clarence is totally enthralled with you, he wants to set up another meet.'

Bella smiled and said, 'Is his wife invited this time?'

'I doubt it after that spat, good God, I thought she was going to flea him alive with that riding crop.'

He raised his hand, lifted Bella's skirt and started to massage her upper thigh. Bella opened her legs slightly to allow him more access. He didn't need a second invitation and strummed her thong with enthusiasm. Five seconds later his fingers pulled the skimpy material aside and were massaging her vagina. Bella shook her head and tits as her clitoris became wet, Sir James increased the pressure and his fingers slid through to her nub. Bella drank her Chardonnay and saw Belinda return braless from the ladies.

'Talk about the relief of Mafeking.' thought Bella.

Sir James studied Belinda as she stood next to the table with her wet tits pushing through her now terribly translucent blouse.

'God she's beautiful.' he thought.

'Sit down next to me Belinda... there's room for us all on this seat, nudge up Bella.'

Sir James kept the massage going on Bella's clitoris as they nudged up, it was getting wetter and wetter. Bella kept drinking and drinking. Belinda joined her and filled their glasses to the brims. Belinda sat down next to Sir James as instructed; she undid the buttons to her blouse except for the last one. That one was for Sir James's pleasure. She stuck her wet breasts into his face and he responded by licking the centre of her left tit where the nipple would soon harden. It did, pushing its way through the silk material, wanting release. He connected with it, and soon Belinda was feeling the erotic sensations shooting up to her brain from her nipple nerve endings. Sir James calmly undid the last button with his free hand and Belinda's ample breasts were his and his alone.

Chapter 11;

Forsters of Knightsbridge, Dressage outfitters to Royalty;

Belinda and Bella had a lazy breakfast of fresh fruit and Special Jay. The newly made smell of ground coffee lingered throughout the apartment subtly announcing the arrival of the weekend.

'OK Belinda, what have you got planned for us to do today?' asked Bella stretching her hands above her head and yawning.

'Surprise, surprise we're going shopping and not just for thongs and bras, I want to get my horse riding outfit.'

'That sounds a bit specialised, I doubt Asda would stock that sort of stuff. Isn't it a bit posh for you anyway?'

'Probably, Bella, probably, but the Duchess got me into it, and to be honest, I look a million dollars all kitted out. Thinking about it, you would too!'

'Do you think? Is it expensive?'

'Haven't a clue, but then what isn't these days.'

'So where's the shop... do they have a shop or is it just in a barn or something... you know, next to where they keep the horses?'

'We're actually going to Knightsbridge, a place called Forsters, and from what the Duchess tells me the male sales assistants are top notch!'

'Now you're talking Belinda.' as Bella started to clear away the breakfast things.

Twenty minutes later saw Belinda stop in front of what looked like Ye Olde Curiosity Shoppe.

'This is it!' A bell jangled and the two girls walked into the subdued interior.

'Good morning ladies.' said an approximately eighty one year old gentleman dressed in a morning suit from behind a highly polished wooden counter.

'There goes the young male attendants story up in smoke, if I may make so bold, Belinda.' whispered Bella.

'Good morning sir, you've been recommended to me by the Duchess of Epsom.'

'Have we now,' the old retainer smiled, 'then in that case you'd better follow me.'

He led them through a doorway into what was a display room of leather riding gear and stopped at a lift. He slowly jabbed at the button and ushered them inside. It wasn't a big lift and Belinda's and Bella's breasts jostled with each other as they tried to avoid contact with the elderly gentleman's nostrils. They slowly went up three floors to what was labelled 'Lady's Riding Area.'

Belinda thought it was quite apt that the Ladys Riding area was the floor above the Men's Riding area. 'Nice to know we're on top.' she commented to Bella.

The lift stopped and Cedric ushered them through to a central area stocked with everything a lady could want for her riding experience. He pressed a bell, bowed to Bella and Belinda and said,

'The younger gentlemen will be here in a minute or so.'

He wheezed, coughed and went back down in the lift to resume his gatekeeping duties.

'Wow!' thought Belinda, 'they've got everything.' She was brought back to reality by a gentle cough from behind her emanating from a handsome gent dressed in riding clothes, and her favourite, extremely shiny black leather boots.

'Good morning Madam, my name is Adaam and I'm here to serve you. I gather our good acquaintance, The Duchess, has verified you.'

'Yes Adaam,' replied Belinda, 'will you be able to service both my friend and myself, so to speak, or do we need another staff member?'

'Why yes Madam, I'm trained in multi-tasking, it will be my pleasure to assist you both at the same time.'

Belinda smiled; she hadn't had a proper threesome for some time.

A full thirty minutes had passed in the knowledgeable presence of Adaam and Belinda and Bella had now both fully briefed him as to what their needs were. Bella was going simple but effective, whereas Belinda was going aristocracy level. The basic difference apart from quality was the price. Bella was going to spend a grand, Belinda five grand, essentially the difference in their pay grades. Adaam had by now opened the second bottle of champagne, as the girls were thirsty. Bella blamed the two bacon sandwiches she had at the café whilst waiting for the tube.

'Ladies, if I might so boldly ask, do you know your vital measurements, by that I mean apart from the obvious, your, inner leg length, head size, etc. etc.'

Belinda and Bella looked at each other, they knew brassiere sizes and thong sizes, but everything else had passed them by, 6, 8, 10 or on a bad day 12's was all they understood. Anyway, they sold pots and pans... not clothing. They both shook their heads glumly and mumbled their apologies.

'No, please ladies, don't be downhearted,' said Adaam with a winning smile on his face, 'I love this part of the job, I'll just get my measuring tape and we'll get started.' He left the partially enclosed area and came back minutes later with a measuring tape and surprisingly, to Belinda and Bella, a female assistant.

'This is Samantha, she's just here to write down the measurements and fetch and carry the garments from our storage area... really!

'Hi Samantha.' said Belinda and Bella in unison, they looked at each other and giggled, had Samantha ever seen Adaam naked they wondered. Samantha curtsied to them and said, 'Hello.'

She sat down and produced a notebook.

'Madam, you first.' commanded Adaam pointing at Bella in an authoritarian voice. Bella put her champagne flute down, after draining it first of course, and stood up.

'Leg's apart please.' Bella moved her legs apart enough so that she could feel her vagina awakening to the new stance and Adaam competently completed the necessary measurements. He went from the tip of her big toe to the top of her head; there must have been at least over 100 different figures.

'Good,' he said, 'Now Madam, it's your turn.' Belinda stood up and voluntarily took a similar posture to that of Bella's.

Adaam gulped and took Belinda's inside leg measurement.

'I'm sorry Madam,' he said, 'your leather trousers are not helping give me a true figure, would you mind removing them... sorry to ask and all that.'

'I thought you'd never ask,' said Belinda, 'I certainly wouldn't sell you a set of expensive pots and pans without seeing your granite worktop!'

Adaam smiled and wondered what the hell she was going on about, he hadn't asked her to strip... just yet.

Meanwhile Bella laughed and said, 'Typical Belinda, always referring things to work!'

Adaam nodded, still puzzled and pressed on. Belinda had by now kindly removed her dark black trousers and thong. Adaam studied her vagina with professional interest. He gently traced the small track of dark pubic hair down to the top of her labia with his forefinger. There he stopped and placed the measuring tape, its metal end was cold and Belinda flinched.

'Apologies Madam, I'll warm the fucking thing up, pardon the coarse language of course.'

Belinda smiled, 'No don't mind me; please carry on.'

Two minutes later and with not a small amount of pleasure imparted to Belinda, Adaam had moved on to her legs and feet.

'I'm sorry Madam, I'm having a bad morning, would you… could you remove your stockings and your heels again… please, the measurements will be so much more accurate, and to be honest the quality of merchandise you are investing in demands the highest of tolerances.'

Now this was the sort of talk Belinda understood, she had always believed that the more you paid, the better the service you would receive and that would reflect in the quality of the goods. Steele's Pots and Pans was also that sort of operation and as their International Sales Director, Belinda would make sure it stayed that way.

Her thoughts came back to the present.

'Madam, did you hear me?' said Adaam.

'Get your kit off Belinda.' said an enthusiastic Bella now fully reclined on a white leather settee with another full flute of champagne in her hand.

'Sorry Adaam, I was daydreaming.'

'Don't apologise Madam, I'm glad I'm relaxing you sufficiently to have a daydream!'

Adaam smiled;

Belinda blinked;

Chapter 12;

The fitting bit;

Twenty minutes had passed; Bella had by now started her third bottle of Champagne and was enjoying every moment of Belinda being systematically stripped by Adaam. He had left no stone, as they say, unturned. Even the clasp retaining her long black hair had been removed; he had explained this was essential in order to get the exact riding hat measurements. Samantha had been sent to the stock rooms for the required garments and would return he said in about thirty minutes, she would be extremely busy he had added.

The diversity of Belinda's and Bella's clothing requirements would challenge Forster's reputation, Adaam had added, albeit, guardedly. The brassiere and special riding thong requirements were, to say the least, 'unusual'. Belinda asked why this was so.

Adaam answered, 'It's down to demand really, as you know through the Duchess we get a lot of young aristocratic ladies through these doors. Quite simply, they're poorly built, by that I mean, little food, too much alcohol, spoiled to death and with little back bone. To us that means' small brassiere and panty sizes... there's little demand for the thong... which is a pity. Personally speaking, it's all I wear, especially when I'm riding.'

Belinda and Bella were intrigued.

'Are you wearing one now?' asked the naked Belinda, simply.

'Why yes Madam, I certainly am!'

'Let's see it.' said Bella warming to her new task of undressing Adaam.

Adaam pulled down the heavily elasticated white jodhpurs he was wearing and revealed a delicate black thong with red trim.

'Do you sell these here?' asked Belinda.

'Why of course Madam, its company policy to only wear what we sell.'

'I understand,' she replied, and what about the socks?'

'Socks, Madam?'

'Yes, the garment you wear between the bare foot and the black leather riding boot?

'Aaah,' he said knowingly, 'you mean the hose.'

'Yes I do, how stupid of me to forget, yes, let's see your hose!'

Adaam sat down and lifted his left leg.

'I apologise, I would ask Samantha to do me this service, but she's not here, Madam could I ask you to assist me?'

'Why yes of course, I'm an old hand at this kind of thing.' thinking of her evening with the Duchess only a week ago.

Belinda quickly and efficiently helped pull Adaam's two riding boots off his feet. In doing so he had a magnificent view of her naked ass and splayed lower vagina. She in return turned round to inspect his hose. It was unremarkable, but she now had his boots off.

Bella stood up and said, 'Could I feel the texture of this hose, as I might want to purchase some?'

'Certainly madam;' Adaam pulled the hose off his feet and handed one each to Bella and Belinda. Bella couldn't resist a sniff, 'God that smells good.' she exclaimed to Belinda. Belinda put Adaam's hose up to her nose, smelt it and said,

'Maltings... Irish... Bushmills, situated on the north Antrim coast.' she could even smell the sea weed in the air.

Adaam blushed, 'I've just returned from holiday, I remember we had a skin-full in the Distillery yesterday lunchtime, but I never thought it would be so obvious.'

'Don't worry, we're not MI6, my dad's a wine and spirits buff and he's trained me well.' replied Belinda whilst patting Adaam's naked thigh.

Adaam stood there with his thong performing at ninety three percent. To Belinda and Bella it was obvious that his red jacket and white shirt were the next to go.

'Now,' said Belinda, 'explain to me about these red jackets... why are they sooo expensive.'

Adaam warmed to his task, 'Well simply put they cost a fortune to make... this is all moles hair and as you may well know, moles ain't big, they also don't occur naturally in red, which means a dyeing process is involved. It alone costs a fortune, but the good thing is, they never fade or crease. They will last a century, which is why sales are so small, and why we may struggle with your 'larger in the bust' sizes.'

Bella looked at Belinda, 'I like this shop, first time I've ever been described as having 'larger breasts' in a clothing store. Adaam, could I possibly feel your jacket?'

'Why yes of course.' Adaam quickly pulled off his red riding jacket and gave it to Bella who threw it into the corner of the room, it fell roughly to the floor, but didn't seem to crease.

Belinda moved her hand up to Adaam's chest and started to open his shirt buttons. He stood still waiting, Bella removed the shirt and tossed it in the general direction of the jacket. Adaam was totally naked except for his thong. Belinda took it and pulled it down, his already extended cock sprung fully to attention, ready for duty as a dedicated Forsters employee should be.

Bella whistled, 'Not bad for a lad; would you say he was hung like a red London bus Belinda?'

Belinda nodded, crouched and put her mouth over his cock. Adaam pushed into her throat, his foreskin began to retract as Belinda gained traction on the moving penis. Adaam grabbed the still fully clad Bella and pulled her to him. He kissed her deeply and she started to tear off her clothing.

The two naked girls worked hard on Adaam. He likewise was no slouch, with a hand on each of their breasts he was giving as good as he got. The action got more intense, the girls started to gently perspire and Adaam fell onto the white settee. Belinda reached for a glass of champagne. She was thirsty and wanted a drink before she started on Adaam's toes. Meanwhile Bella had spotted Belinda spitting out Adaam's cock and she straddled him immediately. He responded with gusto and was fucking her hard. Bella felt she was a cowboy on a bucking bronco, quite apt for the shopping experience they were having she thought.

It all stopped before Belinda could refill her second glass, Samantha had returned from the stock rooms. She quietly coughed and Adaam sat up. Bella had no option but to withdraw and fell back only partially exhausted onto the floor.

Adaam said, 'Thank you ladies for bearing with us whilst Samantha sourced the garments and accessories. Now that we're all undressed, let's see if these items fit you, please forgive my cold hands. Adaam competently dressed Bella and Belinda and after only a few minutes they looked like the real thing.

Adaam stood back and surveyed his handiwork. For sure, Bella's outfit didn't look as expensive as Belinda's but it still did the job, he felt she looked extremely attractive. Belinda however with her long black hair, legs to die for and oval breasts that shouted out 'hold me tightly' was something else. He knew for certain that his dress skills would make her stand out at the next horse jumping club dinner she attended, and that meant she was in the A-class. The English aristocracy would love her to bits.

Chapter 13;

Up, up and away;

Bella and Belinda were standing in line to board the Texas bound flight watching the aircrew walk onto the plane.

'That's Hazel, the blonde, second from front with the sexy cap.'

'Bit of a stunner Belinda if you ask me' said Bella.

'Tits to die for Bella!' said Belinda.

'Not better than ours... surely not Belinda!'

'I'll let you be the judge of that!'

'Promises, promises Belinda,' said Bella laughing.

Unbeknown to Belinda, Hazel had both her and Bella upgraded from economy comfort class to VIP. It was their first big surprise of the day, and Belinda started to muse that it wasn't their last. Champagne was the de rigour and as they were both thirsty, it wasn't long before two bottles were consumed.

'Where's your pal Hazel,' asked Bella, 'shouldn't she have surfaced by now?'

'Probably flying around some big thunderstorms,' replied Belinda still thinking about her time with the Countess Zara which truth be told she still hadn't fully recovered from. Belinda couldn't believe how amazing her time with her was and she had to arrange an introduction to the Duchess ASAP.

'Well let's hope she turns up soon before I get too pissed.' said a still thirsty Bella.

'As you're drinking enough for two people, Bella, that might take some time!' replied Belinda. They both laughed and ordered another bottle of bubbly just to be on the safe side.

As the plane flew on they snoozed in the luxury of the big wide reclined seats. When awake they drank champagne and waited patiently for Hazel's break time. It actually came sooner than they expected with Hazel awakening them both with an urgent shaking of the shoulder hissing,

'Follow me to the forward toilet area.' Belinda and Bella did as instructed and watched in disbelief as Hazel unlocked what to them looked like an emergency exit. She calmly pushed down the large cream coloured handle and pulled the door open. A small spiral staircase led up to a cramped area above the first class passenger section, five identical doors all about four feet in height were laid out in front of them. Their only identification was B1 to B5. Hazel headed immediately to B3, and went inside. Belinda and Bella followed. To their surprise the whole area was a large bed... nothing else, but it was big enough for three people... B3. Belinda asked the obvious question,

'Does B3 mean Bonking capacity for three people?'

'Exactly,' replied Hazel, 'Do you think us air crew are stupid? Space is of the utmost in any aeroplane and no employee would ever think of using a B5 area for only four people.' Belinda and Bella nodded their heads, it indeed made sense, but how often did a B5 area get used, or for that matter a B4 area and could they be invited the next time it did? Thankfully they never wanted to be in the B1 area, was it for males only they both thought. It somehow seemed to them both very lonely.

Hazel looked at her large silver watch with its fluorescent green hands,

'Come on guys, I've only got fifty one minutes left of my break, let's have some action!' Bella and Belinda both dived on Hazel, she screamed in delight gurgling,

'It's OK, we're soundproofed!' She soon lost her uniform and pretty quickly her undergarments which to Belinda seemed quite sexy for standard issue airline employee clothing. She mused, 'they must have an enlightened buyer to be purchasing this lot... must make contact.' Hazel was stripped naked in ninety seconds and Bella paused to assess her tits.

'Belinda, I think you may be correct, though I will need Giselle to qualify my assessment.'

'Surely not,' replied Belinda, and with a flying leap Bella landed on top of Belinda and with Hazel's help had her stripped off in a record forty seconds. That left Bella still somewhat attired, but Hazel had other ideas and went on the attack. Bella soon succumbed and the three girls were now stripped for action, so to speak.

And then the real fun started, Belinda grabbed Hazel's breasts and started preening them with her fingers, it was a very slow touch, much in the style of an Irish Wake... a lot of feeling without much emotion, or perhaps a lot of emotion without much feeling.

Whatever, Hazel soon started to respond and then Bella started on her vagina, gently at first but with enough pressure from Bella's two fingers to create a growing feeling of need. Hazel threw back her long blonde hair and opened her legs wider, arched her back increasing the pressure on her breasts from Belinda's now deft touches and started to moan seductively.

Belinda eventually straddled Hazel placing her vagina over Hazel's face and slowly went down on her. Hazel responded by licking firstly her lids and then finding the clitoris. The initial small amount of fluid being produced was greedily licked up by Hazel who smacked her lips hungrily from time to time. Bella had in the meantime placed her ass in Belinda's face and her mouth over Hazel's clitoris with her tongue soon making a huge impact. That left Belinda sucking Bella's vagina as best she could, but with a little assistance from her fingers she was soon able to kick start a flow of wetness. The three girls remained silent as they each enjoyed the thrills of oral sex.

'Time to swop over.' said a tiny voice deep under Belinda. It was Hazel and as she was the only one on a strict timetable she had kept tabs on the time by checking her large fluorescent watch.

'Fair enough.' replied the other two. Belinda took Hazel's place and Bella Belinda's, leaving Hazel free to move to Bella's old position. They all got comfortable and started again. This time the juices really flowed and it wasn't long until Hazel decided they would swop over again.

'I don't want you guys to dry up,' said a panting Hazel, 'that would be truly unthinkable!' Bella and Belinda nodded as they took up their positions for the last time. Whilst they had never experienced a session quite like this 40,000 feet up in the air, they were willing to accept Hazels superior knowledge, that it could be possible that one or heaven forbid all three could dry up at any time. No doubt one of the risks of air travel they didn't tell you about!

Hazel needn't have worried, Belinda and Bella were made of stern stuff and they lasted the pace, perhaps working in the pots and pans business had given them some Teflon coating. A bit of rough air turbulence initiated a message from the captain asking everyone to fasten their seat belts which saw Hazel loose her concentration. She slapped Belinda's ass and shouted,

'That's it girls, thanks for the party, especially the drinks, let's meet again soon.' They all quickly dressed and headed back down to their seats. Belinda and Bella ordered another bottle of champers as they reckoned they needed to replace their liquid levels. After all Jim Stirling was getting closer with every hour; Belinda needed some time to practice her new cervix techniques. She wasn't going to easily waste the expensive six hours she'd spent with a personal trainer to not finish mastering the skills which would clinch the biggest pots and pans deal of her career.

Chapter 14;
Texas, USA;

Bella and Belinda arrived at their hotel late in the evening, but not too late to get some food and a final drink from the bar. Giselle had been in touch with the Stirling organisation and had managed to get them both into separate suites on the seventeenth floor of Stirling's own company hotel, just two floors down from the penthouse where Jim resided when he was in town. Belinda was pleased with the arrangements, she had Bella within shouting distance and Jim's organisation was housed below them in the large office park which was the nerve centre of Stirling's operations.

After a simple supper of steak, hash browns and lots of red wine... they didn't have a Chardonnay in stock, Belinda and Bella moved to the bar. Even at this late hour it was pretty busy, with company executives finishing off deals and organising future meetings. Being complete strangers in town they were on their own. They hoped to meet Jim Stirling the next day before their meetings with the various management people but that hadn't yet been confirmed with his office. Bella sat on a bar stool and surveyed the room.

'Lots of tycoons here Belinda, do you think we'll make the grade?'

'Of course we will, all we have to do is stick to our appointments and show our fantastic assets!'

They chinked glasses and laughed, that after all was what they were good at... customer satisfaction.

Being two attractive females in a mainly male dominated environment it wasn't long before they were joined by some sharply dressed executives. As this was primarily an in house business hotel there would be no funny business, so the girls felt relaxed. Belinda introduced herself and Bella and explained why they were in town. One of the executives said he'd heard good things about the products and that he was on one of the quality teams they would be meeting with, over the next two days. The only disappointing news was that as far as they were aware, Jim Stirling himself wasn't around. He was still on a business trip to Brazil where they were expanding rapidly, but were encountering worrying exchange rate fluctuations. Jim had decided to make a visit himself to ascertain the depth of the problem.

'But hey, we're still here!' said one of the other executives seeing Belinda's face fall. 'Jim doesn't do it all you know, provided he's given his intent then you're home free and as far as I know you guys are on a meet and greet visit. I'm in contracts and it's all tied up on our side. Now what are you drinking?'

The girls replenished their glasses and chatted amiably with the executives for the next twenty minutes. It was then time for some much needed sleep, they made their excuses and promised to meet them again tomorrow night. On the way up in the lift Bella said,

'What do you think Belinda… is it a done deal?'

'I'm not sure, I was hoping Jim would be here to help us tie it up tight, we may have more work to do than they're letting on, but that's for tomorrow.' Belinda grasped Bella's breasts as the lift whizzed the sixteen floors upwards. Bella responded by inserting her pink red tongue into Belinda's open mouth. They locked on, and as the lift slowed to their floor, re-avowed their passion for each other. The lift doors pinged, opened and the two girls parted on their corridor each going to their own rooms. Belinda decided to sleep naked, she didn't like the air con turned on even though it was warmish in the room. She lay down and worked on her strategy, Jim not being around was bad news.

Belinda stirred in her sleep, she slowly awoke to a persistent knocking at her room door. Her mind started racing, this was the States, her father had always told her you never opened your hotel door to any stranger... as a senior executive she could be kidnapped. The knocking continued, Belinda picked up a metal vase from the table and tiptoed across to the door.

'Who is it?'

'Open the door, it's me…. Jim Stirling.'

Belinda blinked;

She slowly unlocked the door suspecting some sort of trick, but outside stood a gently perspiring Jim Stirling.

'Hi ya Belinder… good to see ya, thanks for making the trip!'

'Jim… but I thought you were in Brazil?'

'Can I come in, I feel kinda stupid standing out here and I can see you're dressed for me!'

Belinda suddenly realised she was bone naked, carrying only a vase. She opened the door fully and beckoned Jim to come in. She pulled her bathrobe off a nearby chair which was conveniently positioned in the far corner of the room and invited Jim to sit down.

'Thanks Belinder, I thought you were never going to open up and I didn't want to call my security just for an access key.'

'Sorry about that, but we just got in late this evening.'

'We?' Jim asked.

'Yes, I've brought Bella to help with some of the admin work... I hope that was OK?'

'Nope, that's perfect, she's a great gal and I want her to meet some of my top people. But hey, what about you... how's the pot and pans business?' Jim smiled.

'Actually Jim, it's great, and that's why we're here to see you... we want to consolidate our business affairs.' Belinda started to flex her cervix, she needed about five minutes of exercises to get it into peak condition, just the way her personal trainer in London had taught her.

Jim walked over to Belinda and gently took off her robe with his massive hands. His large thumbs rubbed her nipples and Belinda shuddered with expectation... or the lack thereof, she wasn't quite sure which.

'Belinder, I need to tell you something, something serious that you must keep private, it's essentially between you and me.'

Belinda nodded her acceptance and thought,

'Surely he hasn't lost his penis completely through some wasting disease... even all her new exercises couldn't deal with that problem.'

'In fact,' Jim continued, 'Can I show you rather than tell you... somehow it's easier for me.'

Belinda half closed her eyes, she felt she couldn't take much more of this... she needed to know the worst.

Jim slowly undressed leaving his pants until last. With a final long look at Belinda he slowly took them off, now dressed only in a black thong he showed Belinda his secret.

'Remember Belinder, this is between you and me... literally.'

Belinda nodded, she didn't know what to say, all she could do was reach forward and pull down Jim's thong. She was shocked, what could she say, how could she tell Jim what she felt, tears trickled down her face, and Jim held her tenderly in his arms.

'There, there, Belinder, you can learn to deal with this as I have, it's only a matter of time and getting used to new circumstances... that's all that matters!'

Chapter 15;

Jim's secret;

'Jim, I'm so pleased for you, how did you do it?'

'Well it wasn't easy, firstly I had to come to terms with my problem…. not that I saw it as a problem, but I have to kinda admit that my meeting with you, in that maze, resolved my mind to do something positive. I'd been doin' some research over the previous few months and a doctor pal of mine kindly came up with the solution. Not that it was inexpensive mind you. Anyways, the only place to go was Brazil so I signed up with the clinic in the Amazon and just went for it.'

'An untried medical procedure in Brazil… you were very brave Jim.'

'Yeah, and very, very desperate, and I still am.' Jim started to caress Belinda's breasts. Belinda pulled him over to the bed and started to stimulate his monster dick with her hand. As she did so, some of the skin fell to the ground… Belinda quickly backed off.

'Jim, I'm sorry, have I damaged it?'

'Nope…. It's all part of the restorative process, I must admit I felt like a snake when I first got out of the operating theatre, there was loose skin all over the place.'

Belinda blinked;

Could she really accept any amount of loose skin inside her vagina? Perhaps it would attach itself to her and start to regenerate…. could

94

she live life with a monster dick like Jim's? She resolved to go for it... what the fuck, she'd always liked the name Richard anyway.

Belinda started to give Jim a blow job, she made sure she started with plenty of saliva; she still didn't have the confidence Jim did that the whole thing might just dissolve like an ice lolly. However it was fine, the few bits of loose skin that did get stuck in her teeth would easily be dislodged when she brushed and flossed in the morning. Now suitably aroused, Jim felt ready for a bit more action. He slowly pushed Belinda back onto the bed, spread her willing legs and entered her. He groaned in ecstasy, he at last experienced what every single other man in the world had been enjoying. It felt fantastic.

Slowly, inch by inch Jim continued his penetration of Belinda's vagina. He felt her cervix muscles expand as he pushed through to her ovaries. Belinda exhaled and thought she could have saved that thousand pounds on a personal trainer if she'd known about Jim's op. Never mind, it was all for the good, she could lie back and enjoy the ride.

Once Jim had reached full penetration he started to gyrate his new cock, he took it easy at first, he didn't really want it to detach itself inside Belinder... or, he suddenly thought, any other female for that matter. Wow... that was more like the old Jim Stirling, at last his confidence was returning. With a leap of faith and a strong desire to fuck Belinder, Jim quickly got into his rhythm. After a few seconds he threw caution to the winds and really got stuck in.

Belinda too was waiting for disaster, she just couldn't help but think what the emergency ward team would say when she was stretchered through to casualty. She would obviously be conscious; did she have the guts to explain what surgical procedure was needed? God, she thought, how do I get into these situations, why me and not Bella or Giselle?

Jim kept fucking, Belinda flexed her vagina lightly, she wanted Jim to fully complete his experience and thought he had had enough thrusting for his first trip out. It happened quickly, too quickly for Belinda and suddenly she was swimming in a sea of pale blue semen. Jim's big cock, now so handsomely matched with his big balls had exploded. Jim was swaying all over the place, Belinda caught his stocky arms and held him firm, whilst orgasming herself. A load roar engulfed the room, Jim Stirling had come! He slumped onto the bed beside Belinda and gasped for air. After about a minute his breathing subsided and Belinda wiped the sweat and tears from his face.

'Belinder... that was just dandy!'

Belinda laughed in relief, she got up and inspected Jim's nether regions for any signs of permanent damage. Apart from the copious amounts of light blue semen everything seemed to be subsiding nicely. His new equipment was lying back in its proper place and even the foreskin had automatically resumed its protective position.

'Jim, I know this is a dumb question to ask just now, but why is your semen fluorescent blue?'

'Well Belinder, money isn't really a problem… you see we have this new utensil supplier who's going to make us so much money I might as well spend some of it. The blue semen package wasn't much of an add on… but it was really expensive so I figured it was sort of unique.'

Belinda fell back in amazement and guffawed, Jim Stirling was certainly quickly becoming her type of guy, and the little reference to business matters had not gone unnoticed.

'Jim, you are amazing, how do you do it?'

Well it's all about having good friends and associates… and the odd girlfriend just like you!'

Belinda smiled, agreed and said,

'Fancy another test run?'

'Why not Belinder, hey thinkin' about it, let's do it doggy style this time.'

Belinda got onto all fours and Jim positioned himself just right for his second foray of the night. Again he slowly entered Belinda's pussy, he felt like a man revisiting the house where he had grown up as a child, everything was the same, but different, he was now grown up, a fully matured male. Once he'd made sure Belinder was comfortable he started to thrust. This time Belinda felt more reassured with Jim's massive penis firmly penetrating her. She gently repositioned her ass to give him greater access and satisfaction, truth be told, this time she wanted to orgasm before Jim. All that light blue semen exploding over her could be off putting to a girl, but she didn't want to deflate Jim too much on his first night out. The pace picked up, Jim's cock was rubbing her clit just right and Belinda gave into nature, not once but twice before the inevitable blue ejaculation cut across her dreams.

They both flopped back onto the bed and fell asleep exhausted. This time, Belinda didn't even blink.

Chapter 16;

 A bit of Spaghetti sauce;

Breakfast was a thoroughly American affair... maple syrup, beautifully overcooked crispy bacon, eggs and to die for waffles.

Jim's PA, Sydney, approached the girls.

'Hi, you must be Belinda, and you're Bella.' said the extremely pretty and petite Sydney. 'If y'all finished eating, then just follow me to your first meeting.'

Bella swigged down the last of her coffee and with Belinda in tow followed Sydney to the lifts. Once they were inside Sydney delicately opened the top button of her blouse, puffed out her cheeks and punched the 12th floor button,

'Sorry it's so hot in here guys, I'll get maintenance onto it as soon as I deliver you to your first meet.'

'Have you got an itinerary for us Sydney... you know, a schedule?' said Belinda in a professional tone of voice. She was obviously a bit miffed Sydney had stopped at the first blouse button and then had quickly punched the 12th.

'Sorry Belinda, why I sure have.' Sydney passed over a pale blue folder to them each. Two seconds later Bella let out a little sigh of triumph.

'What's up Bella?' Belinda asked.

'Not to offend, but I'm dining with Jim tonight.... are you with us Belinda?'

Belinda quickly looked down the page, turned it over and shook her head... she couldn't understand it, she was completely free from 6.00pm.

'No, I'm free all evening.'

'Well,' said Bella, 'Gives you an opportunity to catch up on a good nights sleep!'

The lift stopped and Sydney ushered the two girls through to a meeting room

''Mr Stirling will be joining you shortly along with his Chief Executive Hank Skank.' she informed them. With that Sydney left, returning to her duties on the 19th floor.

Belinda had heard of this Hank Skank. He was reputed to be a hard ball type of guy and with a name like that you could understand it. Of Swedish descent he was a second generation immigrant, blue eyes, blonde hair and a lean stature. More to the point, he reputedly had no problem in telling Jim where to stick his ass if he felt a wrong decision was being made by the owner. It was starting to look like it was as essential to win him over as it had been Jim.

Five minutes later Jim and Hank entered the room. Hank introduced himself and Jim asked him what he was doing that evening.

'The usual Jim, out with the high rollers... why do you ask?'

'Well I've got a business appointment with Bella on some paperwork protocols we need to set up between the two companies, so I would appreciate it if you could take Belinder under your wing... so to speak.'

'Why sure Jim, Belinda, that would be an honor. Can you get yourself to my office for 6.30 and we'll go catch a game at the Stadium, the Krankies are in town and Ron and Nancy have promised me tickets. Don't worry, it's soccer, you know, football to you guys so you'll enjoy it. No problem with a fourth ticket, Ron owns the place!'

'Wow Hank, that's great, I love seeing a few balls being kicked around, I'll be there on time.'

'That's settled,' said Jim, 'and you Bella, had better not be late!'

'Yes sir!' replied an extremely relieved Bella, she didn't like pulling rank over Belinda, but Jim had played it perfectly.

Sometime later Hank was sat opposite Belinda in a very discreet and quiet Italian restaurant.

'Too bad the Krankies got beat, but as they say you can't win 'em all!'

Belinda nodded, and waited, she'd established during the football match that Hank was attracted to her, but he hadn't made any physical moves on her. She also didn't want to manipulate the situation... this guy was a tough dude, and by being a bit too over familiar she could ruin the whole Stirling deal. It was best for him to make the running... if there was any running to be made. Belinda just waited.

The waiter handed out the menus and Belinda chose a seafood starter followed by Spaghetti Bolognese.

'Very, very good choice Belinda, and might I add, a very brave one... these guys do the best Spaghetti sauce in all of Texas. In fact I'm going to join you.'

Hank ordered a carafe of Chianti house white to go with the seafood and his favourite red, a big traditional Chianti, with the Bolognese.

'Now, where were we?' Hank's hand settled on Belinda's knee. Belinda calmly took it and moved it higher and under, her evening gown utilising the long split in its centre.

'I think we were discussing spaghetti Hank.'

'Good answer Belinda, and what smooth skin.'

Belinda slowly raised her hand to the clasp at the top of her gown, as she undid it the material fell to each side, still nicely retained by her erect nipples but letting her cleavage show.

Hank sat back in his chair, his eyes still fixed on Belinda's chest and removed his hand from her thigh as the waiter served the first course. It was needless to say delicious.

They quickly finished the white and Hank got Belinda ready for the big red he had ordered. He felt his pants tighten in the groin region and he knew he was going to enjoy his Bolognese sauce. Minutes later the waiter served the spaghetti and left the sauce for Hank to dish out.

Hank took the big ladle and served. It wasn't too bad a serve considering he didn't have a clue about tennis. Belinda twirled the spaghetti with her fork like the professional she was, dunked it in the sauce and got stuck in.

Once Hank had assuaged his appetite and poured them both two more bottles of red wine he stared at Belinda.

He had an interesting technique and one Belinda was keen to bring back to Europe, though perhaps not for use inside a, by now, busy Italian trattoria. Hank quietly ripped Belinda's evening gown in two completely exposing her thighs and pussy, but didn't remove it. He then took the ladle and trickled the now cooled sauce over Belinda's breasts watching it slowly make its way down to her navel. After about two minutes it stopped and pooled at her shaved vagina. Once he had a big enough reservoir he carefully opened her vaginal lids and let the sauce do its work. Belinda studied the operation closely, did it require just gravity, or was it the sauce that did the flowing of its own accord. She decided to question Hank later on this technical matter.

Hank slightly pushed back the table, got onto his knees and licked Belinda clean, being careful to leave no area of her body 'unwiped'. He made no sexual advance whatsoever apart from the duties his tongue had to make and Belinda smiled feeling very puzzled. There was certainly now no need for a body massage in the next day or so. However, she was careful to compliment Hank on his capacity for janitorial duties, something she hadn't expected from a very senior exec.

'Why thank you Belinda, I guess it was all those vacation jobs I did when I was a student. Now let's pass up on dessert, order some real Italian sausage and we'll eat it back at your room.'

Belinda fiddled with her dress, making it decent for the taxi ride back to the hotel whilst Hank ordered the sausage and two more bottles of wine. Belinda was bemused and thought things were not going at all to plan with this very strange man. It was looking like he was one of those rare breeds, someone who made sex through the use of food... how exciting and somewhat unusual... what else would she learn tonight?

Hank softly shut Belinda's hotel room door behind them. He took the package of hot sausage and laid it out on its silver foil wrapping on the bedside table. Next he took Belinda's ass in his hands.

'You sure are a pretty one Belinda,' he murmured. 'Can I strip you... and fuck you...?'

'Hank, you were so skilful with that Bolognese sauce I'd love to experience what your big waffle could do to me?' Hank grinned and removed his clothes; he liked girls who could talk dirty. With one hand he ripped Belinda's evening gown off her. Completely naked Belinda stretched herself out on the same bed where Jim Stirling had test drove his new cock just the previous night.

Belinda took Hank's hand and handed him another piece of Italian sausage. He wolfed it down and stuck his rising cock into Belinda's vagina. She moaned softly, Hank belched and stuffed another piece of Italian into his mouth whilst fucking Belinda hard. Belinda relaxed her cervix, now she had gotten Hank where she wanted him; she was going to prolong his experience. Besides, he had another two pieces of succulent yet substantial sausage still to go. He was a man who played hard ball in his business affairs, well... Belinda would play hard ball with him in her arena, a sexual arena the like of which he had never before encountered.

Chapter 17;

A bit of Spaghetti sauce;

The 10.30am boardroom meeting was short and Jim concluded the business by saying,

'Belinder, Bella, it sure has been a pleasure having you guys around this week. Hank and I have truly enjoyed your company and we want to confirm the new deal between our two companies.'

Belinda and Bella shouted "Hooray" in their cute English accents and kissed the two men on their cheeks.

'Hank, is the chopper laid on for the ranch?'

'Yes Jim, Virgil confirmed he'd be here in forty minutes.'

The large executive helicopter landed on its helipad outside Jim's penthouse suite. The party now including Sydney ran across the windswept concrete. Thirty minutes later the chopper swept past the front gate of the Lazy P ranch. It so reminded Belinda of the old Dallas TV series her grandmother used to replay over and over again. Now here she was, she, Belinda, riding with the tycoons, it was truly amazing. Who said being in sales didn't pay!

Hank, dressed only in his board shorts, threw another large rib eye steak onto the BBQ watching the three girls out of the corner of his eye skinny dip in the pool. He looked over at Jim and winked.

'Steak, ass and tits, you can't beat it!'

'Add a beer,' said Jim, 'and I'm on board.' they laughed.

'So Jim, you're 100% with this deal?'

'Yup, I sure am Hank, and I tell ya what, I think we can get a manufacturing licence from these Brits for our operation in Brazil.'

'Early days Jim, but it would fit our plans just fine.'

Jim gently caressed his large cock and looked across the pool at Bella, he liked her a lot, especially as she was shorter than Belinder, she didn't require as much straining for the new boy on the block ... so to speak. Yeah, he could see her in two or three years' time as his VP in Brazil. It would be part of the manufacturing licence deal; he'd make sure of that.

The girls had all put on a bikini bottom for lunch, but remained topless hoping to pick up a bit of a tan on their breasts. Sydney had turned out to be a bit of a stunner once her work clothing had been removed and was the real host of the lunch. Hank served the medium rare steak straight from the BBQ, it was a wonderful interlude from all the business dealings of the last two days.

Too soon it was all nearly over, Jim, Hank and Sydney had to get back to the office for a 3.00pm treasury meeting. The helicopter zoomed off leaving Bella and Belinda sunning by the pool. Jim had insisted they relax before their evening flight and would send Virgil to pick them up around sixish. They lay back on the loungers, closed their eyes and soaked in the sun. Suddenly a deep, husky, but not unattractive Texan voice interrupted their wellbeing.

'Sorry to interrupt ladies, but we're the ranch crew, Mr Stirling instructed us to make sure ya's all wanted for nothing for the remainder of your stay with us.'

A slightly perspiring Belinda looked up as the voice suddenly put its hand on her ample bare breast and removed her bikini bottom with a well-practiced shake. Belinda's tits and nipples protested against the rough calloused skin on the cowboy's hand and her naked vagina moistened in anticipation.

'That's different.' she muttered as she watched Bella's reaction. She too was experiencing a similar scenario to herself from a second ranch hand. Belinda licked her lips, took a swig of beer and put her hand between the rancher's thighs and rubbed his denimed groin hard. The cowboy moaned and pushed his tobacco stained tongue into Belinda's mouth. Belinda responded by tweaking the denim shirt covering his hardening nipples with her fingers. Her vagina soon became wet as the cowboy slowly inserted his middle finger and felt for her clitoris. Belinda groaned more loudly in her English intonation which made the rancher even more aroused.

'Can I get off this lounger?' Belinda gasped the second the ranch hand came out of her mouth.

'Why sure Dude,' he answered, 'But hey what's your name?' as he stripped himself naked and jumped into the pool.

His companion joined him. Belinda looked across at Bella, they both nodded and seconds later jumped in.

'I'm Belinda.'

'I'm Bella.'

'I'm Doug.'

'I'm Chuck.'

With the introductions over Doug took Belinda in his arms, pushed her against the side of the pool and started to fuck her. Bella who was not known for her tardiness, grabbed Chuck and directed him to do the same thing to her.

Belinda's substantial oval breasts with their extended nipples started to take a heavy toll on Chuck's gorged mouth. Her clitoris too was starting to pay for Chuck's initial expert finger attention and was getting wetter by the minute. Meanwhile Bella was spread across the marble steps which lead into the pool and Chuck was pounding her for all she was worth. Bella's orgasm soon became irrepressible and the air was split with the pure sound of an English lady seeking release.

Belinda had gotten used to Doug's rhythm and took the opportunity to assess the cattle hands. They were tremendous specimens, tanned to an inch of their lives with cocks like concrete gate posts. Belinda swore, God she needed this, whilst Jim and Hank had each done a great job in warming her up, to be finished off by a Texan cowboy was one more wish off her bucket list. Belinda threw back her long black hair and settled down to enjoy the ride. It didn't last too long as her juices never mind the pool water were so prolific that Doug wasn't making much headway.

Belinda glanced across at Bella, she was still flat on her back on the pool steps, screaming for all she was worth with Chuck hammering the life out of her. She was so into it Belinda wondered why the entire ranch wasn't making its way across to the ranch house. However Belinda was a realist and she didn't want a gangbang situation happening during her last few hours in the States. With that thought in her mind she reluctantly tightened her cervix and took Dexter to a higher plane. He exploded deep inside her a couple of seconds later and kissed her deeply. The wonderful taste of nicotine, tequila and beer would never leave Belinda's mind for the rest of her life.

The helicopter touched down on time at the helipad and the ranch hands put Bella and Belinda's travel bags inside. They said adios and the chopper took off a few minutes later for the airport... they would be cutting it fine, but they had permission to land five minutes from the runway their BA jet would be taking off from. They felt like VIP's and, perhaps they now were, to the Stirling Organisation at least. Security went smoothly and whilst the two were the last to board, they soon settled down in the large first class seats Bella had upgraded them to on Jim's insistence that morning. Belinda relaxed back into her seat and thought what a job Bella had done, she'd make her in charge of the account at tomorrow's meeting with Tony. Fancy that, Bella, her first Key Account Manager for Steele's Pots and Pans.

Back at the offices Bella went straight to reception and Belinda sauntered up the stairs and walked into her office. She threw her brief case onto the desk and flopped into her swivel chair. Her phone buzzed.

'Giselle here Belinda… hope you had a good flight? Can you pop into Tony's office for a debrief?

'Oh Hi Giselle, yes, lovely flight, I'll be with you in two.'

Belinda emptied her case, picked up the Stirling Organisation orders and sauntered down the corridor.

Tony ran his hand through his longish hair, 'How do you do this Belinda, I mean are you a real person… these purchase orders are staggering. I don't know if we can even fulfil half of them.'

'Tony, he's got well over a 1000 outlets, so even if he only ordered 20 utensils per shop that's an awful lot of pots and pans. We are in with the big boys and we have to get used to this.'

Tony nodded his head, smiled at Belinda and said,

'Your bonus is going to be worth having, that I can tell you.'

'Upon which I need to speak,' replied a now tentative Belinda. 'I have to be completely honest, Bella needs to be rewarded as well, you could say she was the body lotion that lubricated the moving parts that is Jim Stirling.'

Tony looked Belinda directly in the eye, 'What do you need Belinda?'

'We need, Tony, Bella to be our first Key Account Manager, International Sales. She's proved herself to be so capable, I really need her to hang out with these accounts I'm bringing in. Besides which she's good at operating in my style, she'll be able to assist me with the clients without any upsets... she's also got great tits...!'

Tony blinked;

Want more?

Now if you've enjoyed Belinda Blinked 1; and just finished Belinda Blinked 2; then Belinda Blinked 3; will immerse you deeper into Belinda's sexual world of big international business, rich entrepreneurs and the British aristocracy... I promise!

Rocky xx.

Belinda Blinked 1; is also a published book. It's incorporated in the podcast version called My Dad Wrote a Porno now available in Europe on this link....

http://bit.ly/MDWAP

And in the USA on this link....

http://amzn.to/2zjVmmF

Still hungry for more…. then why not let me send you some exclusive Belinda material. I've got some stuff which I didn't have room for in this book and you're welcome to read it. I also sometimes send out a newsletter with info about the main characters, a new book or podcast. It'll keep you up to date on the Belinda franchise and whet your appetite for more!

It's easy, just email me at flintstonerocky@gmail.com and I'll get back to you.

So this is what you get;

1. Material that didn't make this book.
2. A copy of Belinda's pay slip with deductions; Only the British Government has this classified info!
3. An occasional newsletter.
4. Advance notice of what's happening in the Belinda franchise!

Myself, Belinda, Giselle, Bella and Tony would love you to leave us an honest review. It really helps us to maintain our success in the book rankings. Thank you!

Rocky. xxx

You can find Belinda at www.BelindaBlinked.com and

Rocky at www.RockyFlintstone.com

Printed in Great
Britain
by Amazon

31108279R00071